Does the Dog Die?

"An Anthology of 'Canine Horror'"

DOES THE DOG DIE?

AN ANTHOLOGY OF CANINE HORROR

SHADOW WORK PUBLISHING

CONTENTS

These stories are works of fiction. Names, characters, places and incidents are either the product of the author's imagination or are used fictitiously. Any resemblance to actual persons, living or dead, is entirely coincidental.

No part of this eBook may be reproduced or transmitted in any form or by any means, electronic or mechanical, including photocopying, recording or by any information storage and retrieval system, without written permission from the author.

SHADOW WORK PUBLISHING

All copyrights belong to the authors. © 2024

ISBN: 978-1988819488

Edited by: Duncan Ralston

Cover art by Jorge Jaramillo

For Silvio,
The best friend a man ever had.

CHERRY

MEGAN STOCKTON

Cherry had grown to love the dark.

The dark places were the quiet moments in between the chaos and the pain. She had never known anything except peace when the lights were turned off. The moment the bulbs dimmed above her – their twirled skeletons burning briefly like dying embers within their bulbous glass flesh – she knew that there were no more obligations for her. She could pretend there was nothing else, and those moments both lasted forever and no time at all. Some of the other dogs barked all night. Even in the dark they couldn't seem to find peace like she could. Sometimes she worried about them. Hearing their anxious breaths and frustrated voices made her want to join in.

She curled her body tightly against the box in the back of her cage, nose tucked underneath her hocks. She had once watched a dog lay his tail across his own nose and had been so envious... Cherry's own tail had been snipped off with a cigar cutter when she was just days old. She didn't remember it, but she had witnessed the same done to her puppies, so she knew that she must have been born with one too. It was hard to communicate without it... it was hard to portray your *intentions* without a tail. Every dog she met probably felt as though she was wearing a mask: motive unclear, emotionless.

The sound of the dog in the run next to her prevented her from sleeping tonight. His voice was low, a droning whine that she could tell he tried to stifle. They had been bred not to cry, even when it seemed like the only thing left to do at the end of days like these.

She raised her head, eyes adjusting to the dark as she searched for his form in the inky black of the room. Shadows of some of the restless dogs became visible around her, jumping and bouncing against the chainlink loudly as they spun and paced. Then she saw him curled into the corner nearest her. His body quivered, gently vibrating with pain or fear... maybe both. She made a small noise in her throat, a little grunt as though to let him know she was there and she heard him. Her voice was low, gravelly. She had always sounded a little more like a dog than a bitch, despite her feminine build and proportions.

At the sound of her voice, he quieted immediately, body growing still and rigid. Cherry could feel the creeping, cold tension between them. She got to her paws and slowly padded over before dropping back down to her belly beside him. She whined a comforting word, stretching her nose to the small space beneath the barrier to try and nuzzle him.

He suddenly turned on her, and even in the dark she saw the flash of his teeth: ivory spears that wielded white-hot pain and fury and sparks of saliva flying wildly from beneath his curled tongue. She jerked her face away as he collided with the chain-link between them. More spittle flew at her face as his teeth hooked around the metal diamonds. She saw how worn down they were from moments just like this one; dulled and flattened with visible gray at the core, not those sharpened daggers that she thought she'd seen. His eyes were dilated and wide with rage, white rimmed with warning to her. She could smell the rot on him, the way one of his wounds just wouldn't heal. She could smell the fresh blood and fresh piss from when he had thought his life was over. Those moments where the fear is all that you have.

She sat back on her haunches now, watching as his anger and aggression washed away. They were so unpredictable. All of them. Even Cherry herself.

She was from a long line of warriors, a long line of athletes. Her ancestors were the unstoppable, the unbeatable. Man had taken her heirloom of strength, tenacity, and they had corrupted it. They turned them against each other, and they laughed. They exchanged money for their pain and called it heritage. This was what Man did, and it was known.

Her face was soft as she stared at him, watching as he fell onto the ground, his growls fading into breathy cries. She felt pain in her chest and her stomach, but not the kind of pain experienced when fighting. This was a different type of pain that Cherry didn't really understand. All she knew was that it wasn't her own pain, and that it hurt worse than any bite she'd ever experienced.

She dropped onto her belly, scooting towards him once more. His lips peeled back again: exposing the ruined teeth and his black-speckled gums. Cherry sighed in defeat, whining once in hopes that she could appeal to some kind of patience he might have for her. She wanted to be near him, to comfort him. She fell asleep there with her stomach against the cold concrete, and dreamed of plastic bags rolling down a street in the breeze.

A sudden light flooded the pathway between the two rows of cages, encasing the shadow of a Man in the far doorway. Cherry leapt up, scampering to the back of her cage to retreat into what darkness remained. All of the other dogs became quiet.

No one spoke, no one moved.

The Man flipped on an overhead light, and suddenly everything was visible. Cherry immediately became alert, heart pounding in her chest. She knew the hour was late. The most pain came earlier in the day, the most obligation. Anything that happened at this hour though... well, Cherry knew it wasn't good. She took a deep breath, pulling the Man's distant scent to her. She smelled alcohol and weed, car grease, and some kind of savory human food. A second Man entered, this one a Stranger. He started bickering with her Man.

"You're not a real dogman," the Stranger said, showing his teeth and scrunching his nose. It was as much a snarl as any dog had ever shown. "Your dogs are shit, and you're a poser."

Her Man's shoulders dropped some, but it wasn't a submissive gesture. "Yeah, well... Hank wasn't on his game this morning."

"Yeah, there's not an ounce of *game* in that mongrel. He's a waste of space and food."

"Yeah... maybe. I didn't produce him though, I bought him from Dalton. You know I got almost all my stock from him when I was getting started. He was getting sick about that time."

Cherry stepped forward slowly at the mention of the Man named Dalton. Listening carefully.

"Listen, I got a real game dog you can buy off me *cheap*," the Stranger said. "This dog don't know the meaning of the word quit... but what are you going to do about this loser mutt? Everyone's laughing at you, you know that?"

Her Man hesitated, hands twitching at his sides as he played with the exterior seam of his pants leg. "I'll get rid of him."

"You don't have the balls."

"I do."

"Then do it."

There was a pause of confusion, and Cherry found herself leaning forward even more, cropped ears pricked as she listened intently. She saw something black and metal in the Stranger's hand. He held it out towards her Man, who seemed afraid of it.

It was a gun. Cherry knew it was a gun even before they made their approach. A sudden panic overtook her and she had to suffocate a whine in her throat. What were they doing?

"No, dude, what the fuck." Her Man recoiled, but the gun was forced into his hands anyway.

The pair of them walked to the front of Hank's cage, and Cherry looked away. She didn't want to risk making eye contact with either one of them, but she quickly realized they were too hyper-focused on Hank to pay her any mind.

Hank didn't respond aggressively to the Men like he had Cherry. Instead she saw his rear move side to side as his short tail wagged. Her Man hesitated, looking down at the now-pleasant dog before him. Cherry saw the way that her Man's nostrils flared at the aroma of Hank's infection, the way his eyes brimmed with tears at the sight of the dog's wounded state. This Man had never had the constitution for this; Cherry wondered why he insisted. Why didn't they have a yard with a ball, like the dogs on television? Why didn't they take walks on the sidewalk like the dogs she sometimes saw outside?

The Stranger pushed the younger Man forward.

"Do it. Free up the cage, save on the feed bill. Waste of space. You'll have room for a new dog, a *champion*. Nobody will make fun of you anymore when you get this shithole cleaned up and become a real dogman."

"Yeah... yeah. Waste of space," her Man repeated, but his voice held no confidence.

Waste of space.

Cherry didn't think Hank was a waste of space.

The young Man lifted the gun and aimed it at Hank as he approached, his body curling into a soft c-shape. Hank licked his lips submissively, smiling and blinking. He was giving the Men all the signals of docility and trust. The space between his blocky skull and the end of the handgun was miniscule, Hank had all but laid his forehead against it.

Cherry started panting in anxiety, quickly moving to the side of the cage, leaning heavily against the fencing as she whined. All of her instincts told her to be small, quiet, invisible... but something much stronger told her to beg them not to end his life.

In desperation she grumbled in her throat, softening her facial features until she could barely keep her eyes open. Her lips moved to form the smallest *woo*: the sound of a nervous negotiator. Her Man looked at her once, but his hands stayed steady.

The Stranger put his hand on her Man's and shoved gently, and just as the gun made contact between Hank's hazel eyes, the Man pulled the trigger. Hank lurched, and the back of his skull exploded. Hot blood splattered against Cherry's face and she licked the iron-rich liquid from her lips, squinting against what had gotten into her eyes. It tasted like the cage between them: that metallic tang of steel wire. She looked at Hank as he fell to the floor, paddling in a puddle of his own blood and shit. He looked like he was trying to run, and she wondered if anyone had ever escaped Death as it had come for them in those final moments. Cherry had watched so many dogs try.

Hank cried again; he cried in front of the Men like no good dog ever did.

Cherry wished she hadn't come so close. She would wear

Hank's blood on her golden fur for weeks, she would smell his final moments as it was left on the stained pavement for months, she would hear his screams for the rest of her life. She would miss his presence and wish they could have reconciled, she would remember the day that he was born and the way he had nuzzled against her for those precious early weeks of life. Her youngest son.

"Who's this ugly bitch?" The Stranger motioned to Cherry, and she looked up at him. This time she didn't try to avoid his eyes. They were small and too close together. He looked like a rat. She knew what you did with rats if you got ahold of them.

Her Man was shaking; he was still staring at Hank's now lifeless form as he responded. Cherry hoped it haunted him. "I mostly use her for breeding."

"She's got battle scars all over her. She any good?"

"Yeah, she was really good when she was younger."

"There's a fight tonight, downtown at Tobe's. All bitches. I don't think there's much in the way of competition."

"I don't know, man..."

"Pack her up."

Cherry watched as the Stranger took his gun back, stuffing it into his waistband. She wished he'd shoot his own dick off. Her Man grabbed a leash from the wall and opened her door, squatting down level with her face as he snapped the clasp onto her oversized collar. She could have bitten him in the face, but he touched her with a soft hand on the top of her head and she spared him. She was not inclined to be violent towards the Man, no matter how much he deserved it. The curse of the dog was to love Man: the worst of the animals. The selfish, greedy, unreasonable Man did not deserve the love that dog gave him.

He led Cherry down the aisleway, and the rest of the dogs stared on quietly. Some of them looked on with tight-lipped jealousy, hackles raised and muscles stiff. Others licked their lips sadly, looking away with soft brows and dropped ears. At the door Cherry hesitated, looking back at the dark blood that drained from Hank's run.

"Come on, Cherry," her Man whispered, gently tugging on her leash. Cherry's breath caught in her throat at the tension on her collar, and she sighed before giving in and walking on.

She hadn't fought in a couple of years, removed to bear future warriors instead: an equally tortuous career. She enjoyed her offspring while they were young. Those short weeks of infancy were something that she cherished, having to resist the urge to snap at the Men who would come and hold each puppy up by his scruff like they were entitled to them. They would swing them around, a vulgar use of dog's own language: taking the way their mother would carry them out of love and protection and perverting it into something terrifying and aggressive. As the pups began toddling around, they would be encouraged to play rough, to be loud. Then Man indulged the sin of the dog's bloodlust. If they were lucky, they were made to kill small prey. If they were unlucky, they were made to kill each other.

Cherry's nose worked overtime to take in and categorize all of the scents of the street, she hadn't been outside of the dog runs in a long time now. She paused, nose turned up to the sky as she inhaled deeply. The Man reached down and lifted her into the dogbox in the truck bed, and her bones groaned and cracked. She retreated into the box, darkness enveloping her other than what little light came in through the door. The Man stood there, surrounded by the brightness like a holy figure. He stared at her in the back of the cage and gave her a small smile.

"Good girl."

This gentleness was the only reason that she ate the ball of hamburger meat that he threw in there. She wanted to please, she wanted to reward him for his quiet voice and soft features. She knew what was in the meat, not by name but by effect. She could smell it even through the rich aroma of the beef, and she could taste it when she chewed. It made her salivate with nausea, but she knew the sickness would pass and the intense rage would come. It would awaken the monster of her youth: that creature who did not know submission or surrender.

The Man closed the door and Cherry settled down in the quiet dark, and she waited.

———

CHERRY DIDN'T RECOGNIZE the Man pup that she was handed off to at Tobe's house. He was small, both in stature and disposition, and she came to nearly his waist and might have been half his weight. He had been tasked with giving her the pre-fight bath, washing away anything that might have been put into her hair to hurt her opponent. She normally would have enjoyed a nice bath, but as the boy tried to wash her face with the sponge, she resisted. She grumbled at him, pulling her head away as he wrapped his small arm around her neck and wrestled her. He was washing away what little remained of Hank, and she wasn't ready to let go yet.

He successfully washed her, and she shook off, showering him with miniature droplets. She was shaking with excess energy, nervous energy. It was the stuff in the meat, the stuff that made her angry. Cherry would fight without the stuff, but the Man knew that she would fight harder *with* it. The Man pup reached into his pocket and pulled out a small brown cookie that was shaped like a bone. He looked over each shoulder, and when he noted that no one was watching, he offered it to her.

"Good luck, old girl," he said quietly and he leaned down, with no fear, and kissed the top of her scarred head.

Cherry flinched at the contact but didn't move, feeling an involuntary wag of her short tail as he pulled away and moved on to wash the next dog. She was taken to the ring next. There was a sea of Men that were breathing smoke from their lungs and trading handfuls of filthy bills. The ring was just a shallow hole in the ground, with plywood walls and linoleum rolled out for the flooring. The wood was splintered and chipped, stained the color of wine with blood. In the corners were small pieces of broken teeth and torn off nails. The Man lifted her and set her inside behind the scratch line. The instant her toes touched that line, she focused on the dog directly across from her. This went beyond life or death.

The smell of blood and human sweat, the intense pheromones of the other bitch across the ring, the blinding light of the overhead fluorescent bulbs, the drugs coursing through her system. The *instinctual* drive to not only survive, but to overcome. A growl rose up in Cherry's throat and she barked for the first time in years. The Man held his hands around her chest, holding her back as she barked so hard that she bounced on her front feet, froth flying from her mouth as she salivated with desire.

The other bitch was younger, smaller, and Cherry could tell by the way she leaned back into her Man's hands that she was scared. This might have been her first time; it might be her last time.

Someone dropped a handkerchief in the middle of the ring. Cherry saw its flawlessly white figure float through the air like a descending bird, and then when it landed, the Man let her go. She lurched forward out of his hands, jaws parting before she was even close enough to make contact. A feral snarl ripped from her chest. The other bitch hadn't even crossed the scratch line, her Man had to shove her into the ring with his foot. She squealed, body arching and she looked up at Cherry with so much fear that it was intoxicating. The smaller bitch made a decision. She met Cherry in the air, and they turned into a single blur of fur, noise, and teeth.

Blood ran down Cherry's brow from one swift snap of the other bitch's teeth, but she was able to quickly overpower her. The other female had natural ears: beautiful, soft ears that were speckled black. Cherry went for those first, ripping them until they were shreds of tattered flesh. Blood flooded and overflowed her ear canal as Cherry continued her assault. The other female fought with no experience, no strategy. She bit at the air, chewing at any body part that Cherry put in the line of fire.

Cherry pinned her to the ground, jaws wrapped around her throat. She could feel her windpipe crushing beneath her teeth, teeth puncturing her hide like thick fabric. Then they were there, pressed together on the floor, and when the other dog cried...

She felt her self-control break through the veil of drug-induced fury, through the pain and anger and bloodlust she felt an inkling of compassion. The peaceful dark surrounded them, and it was just her and the younger bitch. They were in the world alone and Cherry was causing pain, she was causing suffering. For a moment Cherry saw her own life flash before her eyes. She was a puppy, hanging by her scruff in the hands of a Man. The first time she killed it was a kitten and they put them together in a small box and taunted her with it. Her first fight she was nearly torn apart: she remembered the sight of her own intestines as they fell out of the gash in her abdomen. She remembered the pain of the needles as they stuffed everything back in and sewed her up.

Cherry released her opponent's throat, slowly pulling her head away to look at her opponent eye to eye. The smaller bitch looked up at her, panting and wheezing, blood gathered in bubbles at the corners of her mouth and around her nostrils. Cherry stepped back and the other bitch stood slowly. They stared at each other, both expecting the other to start again. If you hesitated in an instance like this, you were dead. But the two females seemed to understand each other, to agree.

In the crowd, the dogs waiting their turn in the pit started barking.

Chanting.

A Man entered the ring, jumping over the plywood wall as he approached and reached for the other bitch. Cherry jumped into the air, aiming herself directly at his chest. She hadn't jumped like this in years. When she had been young, she had loved to jump up for the flirt-pole, dangling some furry thing for her to grab hold of. Her muscles strained, but carried her onto a collision course with the human.

He was caught off guard by her sudden attack, falling backwards with Cherry on top of him. The back of his head hit the edge of the plywood, and he started convulsing beneath her. Cherry grabbed his throat: the flesh was so much softer and more tender than a dog's. Her worn teeth pierced it like butter and the rich, fatty flavor of Man-flesh filled her mouth. She salivated, using her powerful shoulders to wrench and tear, pulling and chewing until the Man grew still.

It was all stunned silence around her. The Men were quiet, the other dogs were quiet.

Cherry pulled her mouth away from the Man's mangled neck, raising her bloody head to survey the crowd around her. She licked her lips, eyes fixing on the older Man in the crowd that had given her owner the gun that had killed Hank. He was next.

She growled, the noise bellowing and growing into a bay. The other dogs joined in, and chaos began. Cherry and the other bitch clambered over the plywood wall, and leapt into the crowd. Men started screaming as the other dogs joined in the mutiny.

Cherry dove through the forest of legs after her quarry, who was on the move. He tried to push open a door that led into the hallway, but it required you to pull it open instead. Even Cherry knew which way the door swung. He turned back towards her, pressing his back against the door as she lunged at him. He reached up to protect his neck and face, but Cherry wasn't aiming that high.

He left his entire groin wide open. She grabbed the front of his pants in her mouth, biting down until her teeth grinded together with the thick denim in between. If he hadn't been wearing jeans, she would've made quick work of him. She braced her feet, tugging backwards and thrashing. The Man screamed, and it was the most beautiful sound. Her hair stood up along her spine and her tail wagged fiercely behind her. He started punching her in the head, his weak fists only egging her on. The fabric of the jeans squeaked and finally tore free; she saw the seam come apart in front of her, pulling away with his severed dick sandwiched between the denim and her teeth. What was left of the base spurted blood like a clown's prank flower, darkening the fabric of his pants with both urine and blood.

He grew weaker beneath her and she let go long enough to snuffle inside the saliva-soaked pants to find the dick. She made eye contact with him as she chewed the squishy member between her teeth. It was soft and small, juicy and chewy. Cherry watched as he died, the way he had watched Hank die. She wished she could catch his soul as it fled to their human Hell, and she wished she could kill it too.

The sounds of more Men screaming behind her prodded her on, reminding her she had more work to do. She dropped the penis to the floor, and rushed back into the crowd. The next Man on her shit list was none other than the man who owned her.

Cherry watched with joy as other dogs had turned onto their masters, and the Men who were not dead or dying tried to funnel out the one small exit to escape their fate. She saw her Man shoving his way through the crowd, trying desperately to get to the door. She kept her eyes on him, stepping over the gasping body of one dog who was breathing his final breaths. He had been stabbed, holes whistling with escaping air from his pierced lungs, bubbles and froth gathering around his nose. She wanted to comfort him, but there was no time for that now.

She had gained on the Man, the rest of the crowd parting to avoid her snarls and barks. She grabbed him by the ankle, pulling him away with all of the force she had. He screamed, grabbing the legs of other Men as he begged for help. Two Men grabbed his arms, and the tug-of-war ensued. Cherry was being dragged across the floor, desperate to not let them take him from her. She was owed this. Her entire life had been a series of sins that put this man into the red for her. She was here to collect now. She was ready to put him into the black. The quiet, peaceful black.

Suddenly to her left, the bitch she had been fighting earlier appeared, grabbing his opposite leg. Cherry looked at her out of the corner of her eye: seeing her pretty tattered ears swollen with bubbles of blood beneath the flesh. Together, they dragged the Man away and his comrades gave up on trying to save him. The other bitch held tight to his leg as Cherry released her own and crossed to stand over him, biting onto his face.

His screams echoed in her own throat and she swallowed them down, chomping over and over as she felt his skull collapse beneath his teeth. His short fingernails dug against her face and her neck, one of them piercing her right eye and clawing until it went dim with pink starbursts of pain. Then he went for her left, ramming his thumb so far into it that it hurt her nose. Darkness overcame her completely.

She shook her head once, hearing his neck snap. His head became a floppy, deflating ball in her mouth. She chewed again, jaws flooding with the flavor of his blood and the salty tang of cerebrospinal fluid from his fractured skull. She grasped his nose and his soft lips between her front teeth, chewing the pieces off until she was sure he was a peeled skeleton.

Cherry thought she could still feel his soft breath between his teeth. She dropped the Man, unsure if he was dead in body or only in mind but satisfied with his incapacitation. She was unable to see anything now, blinking against her injured eyes. They felt foreign in her sockets: swollen, puffy chunks of damaged orb catching between her lids. She heard another dog bark once, twice. It was a signal. She headed over slowly, testing each step hesitantly. The ground was littered with bodies, both Man and dog.

She came to stand beside the dog that had barked the signal, sniffing the air between them when she realized that there was Man there... but it was the Man pup from earlier. She leaned towards him, softening her facial features to try and signal to him that she was not here to hurt him. The dog beside her growled and Cherry snapped at him, lip curling up and she felt her teeth just barely nip his shoulder. He huffed and she heard his nails click as he walked away.

She understood the other dog's reservation. This Man pup

would grow up to be Man. Cherry had to believe in happy endings though. It was in her nature to believe and forgive.

Well, not everyone.

But she would give this Man pup a chance.

She flinched as his fingers touched her chin, gently scratching.

"You don't want to hurt me do you, old girl?" His voice was small, shaking. She could smell the fear, but it didn't intoxicate her like the screams of the older Men. He stepped forward, she heard his little feet on the floor between them, and he kissed her head again. His lips made a tacky sound on her blood-soaked head, and then her tail wagged gently.

Cherry walked away from him, returning to where she had cached the amputated dick and picked it up to take with her. It was cold now, but the blood was like jelly filling. She heard the sound of at least a dozen other dogs barking, snarling. She heard their nails on the floor. She heard the Man pup scream, and then the room was filled with the sounds of snapping bones, tearing flesh, and the satisfied sounds of the other dogs.

Not every dog was as quick to love as Cherry. This world was a cold one, and not every pup made the cut. She settled down onto the ground, chewing her prize and shutting out the world around her.

It was easier now, without her eyes.

Cherry had grown to love the dark.

Megan Stockton is a horror author hailing from rural Tennessee where she lives with her family and one murderous Anatolian Shepherd named Chigurh. She only kills fictional dogs, but the same can not be said for people.

LESSONS IN DUDEFIGHTING

JONATHAN BUTCHER

They say that humans are a dog's best friend, but they sure as hell aren't mine. I've never liked the hairless fuckers.

The way they scamper about on all fours like insects? And their smell? That claggy, armpit stink that's somewhere between a cat in heat and a puddle of vinegar? I hate it all.

Apparently a full-grown human has the same intellect as a 3-year-old dog, but I often wonder if there's more going on behind those weird goggling eyes. Some canines say that humans make good pets, but if I had my way, we'd cull them all.

That's why I've got no problem with my poodle pal Spot bashing this chubby bastard's cage and laughing at him shivering in the corner.

"You're going to slaughter them, aren't you, Pale Yellow!" Spot cackles, looming over our petrified captive's cell.

Spot had wanted to call him Steve—a stupid, typical human name—but I'd told him that for now, we'll just call them by their fighting colours. These range, like our eyesight, from yellow to blue.

"Crush them with that fat gut!" Spot barks. "Choke them with those big swinging udders!"

"Those are just tits," I tell him. "Male ones don't have udders."

He grins at me. "Pedantic sod, aren't you, Buddy?"

I'm an Alsatian, so I'm not taking insults from a fuckin' poodle. I glare. Spot's mouth retracts nervously and he returns his eyes to the cage.

"We've trained you up good, haven't we, Pale Yellow? My alpha dude."

The pitiful lump of a man stares wide-eyed up at us; a trapped human on all fours, and a pair of free, top-of-the-food-chain dogs on two legs. Pale Yellow has an odd dent in the side of his head, and the ammonia smell wafting from his body makes my sensitive nose recoil. As I watch, he clambers towards us and pokes his face between the bars, sniffing, as though he expects a treat. I bat his dented forehead with my paw, and he yelps.

"Come on," I mutter to Spot. "We've got an event to run."

FROM THE PREMIUM STAND—A precarious, creaking platform made of hastily-nailed wooden beams—I watch Spot address the baying hounds who are filling my warehouse.

"Dogs and bitches!" he yips into the microphone, his ridiculous curls flopping to the rhythm of the words. "Are you ready for a gorefest?"

"Fuck yeah!" bellows a rottweiler, his tongue lashing from his jaws.

"I want blood!" barks a Jack Russel in a plaid shirt, pumping one paw in the air.

My warehouse is a pulsing swamp of scents: wet fur, sour

breath, sweaty arseholes and canine pheromones. A sharper stink drifts from our human combatants.

The audience stands tall on their hind legs around a square of barbed wire. The knotted metal marks out our fighting pit, which we've covered with straw to help highlight the blood. The crowd hoots and hollers, their excitement aided by the illicit coffee, alcohol, and chocolate we've allowed a couple of pooches to deal on the premises. All bets have been laid, and I'm thinking about the money we're raking in.

The animal rights mutts would be horrified if they knew that Spot and I have been helping train humans to annihilate each other. Setting it up was simple: I had the cash, Spot had the connections, and we both had the desire to hold a night of dude-fighting. Now that our first event has arrived, we're in high spirits.

"In this corner," Spot yells. "We have... Yellow!"

Sat on his haunches, the first human combatant has a streak of yellow paint smudged on his chest. He's light-skinned, heavy on the shoulders, and wears nothing but a spiked collar on a leash. He tenses and pops a turd out onto the straw. Behind him, a tough-looking mongrel with a fluffy mane stands on his hind legs holding the other end of Yellow's leash. He jolts his human fighter with an electrified poker, making Yellow squawk.

The audience howls again.

"And in this corner," Spot continues. "We have... Light-Blue!"

Light-blue is a leaner beast with darker skin and his own painted blue smudge across his chest. He stands on his hands and feet looking ready, his eyes bloodshot but alert. I wonder if his owner has pumped Light-blue full of stimulants, because he chews his jaw as he focuses on his opponent, tugging on his leash. His owner, a suave dachshund, stands calmly at the human's side.

The audience is less enthusiastic about Light-blue, perhaps due to his weaker-looking stature, but I've put my money on him. I've always liked an under-dude.

"This first battle doesn't allow for weapons," Spot says. With a wink, he adds, "We'll build up to that!"

The human fighters lock eyes. Light-blue seems wild and untamed as Yellow narrows his eyelids in concentration. Spot and the other trainers taught me a few things about human body language in the weeks leading up to the event, so I can now tell when they are happy, morose, or ready for a fight—and these two are ready for a fuckin' fight.

"Ready!" Spot yells. "Go!"

The owners release the leashes.

Light-blue and Yellow gallop to the centre of the pit.

The crowd yaps its approval.

As the pair grapple, I can see that Yellow has the advantage: stronger, with good breeding, and well broken by his trainer. But when Yellow shoves Light-blue backwards, Light-blue swipes at his opponent's eye.

"Yeah!" I yell. "Gouge it out!"

Light-blue isn't quick enough to catch the man's eyeball, but his ragged nails drag two bleeding lines across Yellow's cheek. In response, Yellow swings a punch—that's dudefighting lingo for when humans twist their fingers into a knot and hit something. Light-blue reels, totters a bit, then grabs Yellow's throat.

"Look at them," Spot growls, surveying the crawling, battling humans and the cheering crowd. "We're going to make bank from this. That kennel you wanted? You got it. And those rare whalebones that you love to gnaw? Take your fuckin' pick."

Light-blue has Yellow on his back now, his wiry strength overwhelming his opponent's lumbering brutality. With one hand pressed to Yellow's face and his forefinger searching for the poor bastard's eye socket, Light-blue uses his other hand to pound Yellow's throat, crushing the bones and cartilage there. As Light-blue's finger punctures Yellow's eye, a gunshot rocks the warehouse.

The cheering stops. All muzzles swing towards the noise. Whatever our attendees see behind them in the dark corners of the warehouse makes them whine, their haunches trembling.

I see nothing so I duck behind the wooden planks of the premium stand, then raise my snout above the line and sniff. Through the throbbing reek of our crowd and our fighters, something new haunts the air. Something musty.

There's another gunshot, then two more, so I raise my head above the planks. Two audience members lie bloody and convulsing on the ground. A flash breaks through the shadows and another blast rings out. The dachshund trainer's nose snaps away from his face in a shower of rich blue blood.

I duck my head and exhale. This isn't my first sight of violence or the first time my life has been threatened. I feel myself slip back into a primitive mindset from way back in our evolutionary chain, before dogs stood upright, used tools, or buried our dead as well as our chew-bones, and before scuttling humans called out from the dreadful dark, attracted by our canine campfires and the waft of cooked meat and bubbling marrow. I feel reptilian again, ready to kill whatever wants to kill me.

"Fuck, fuck, fuck," Spot moans, cowering in the corner of the stand.

I should never have teamed up with a fuckin' poodle.

"Snap out of it," I say, as more bangs and barks shake the building.

The poodle looks at me so feebly that I want to tear his throat out. I don't, because his only sin is that he's pathetic;

whoever is firing these guns is a menace that needs to be stopped.

I hurry down from the premium stand and crouch low behind the stairs. After a thunderstorm of gunshots and yelps, the shooting stops.

I peek my head around to get a better look. With a boom, something white-hot tears through my face. The air glitters with a geyser of blood and teeth, and then I'm wincing, clutching my ripped flesh and fur.

"Come on out, Buddy," a voice calls through my agony. "That was supposed to be a warning shot. I never meant to hit you, but you moved right into it."

Pouring blood from my torn jaw, I wonder: Is it the cops?

Or maybe Fido, stepping on my operation?

No. This isn't their style—an operation from Fido's 'Good Bois' crew would have gone more smoothly, and the police would have been a lot less 'bullety.'

"Come on, I'm serious," the voice calls.

Recognition scampers through my brain. I glance up the stairs to the premium stand. Spot's wet eyes gleam. He shakes his head, poodle-curls bouncing ludicrously.

Resisting the urge to whine in pain, I step out from the stairs, drooling gore.

"Hello again, Buddy."

A familiar St Bernard stands at the centre of the fighting pit, surrounded by corpses. The first two human combatants crouch bewildered and bleeding by her side, while their trainers and the spectators lie still or spasming, riddled with holes. The remaining few attendees cower in fear while four other armed dogs—all golden retrievers, all skinny as hell— stand in the dim background, smoking guns clasped in their paws.

Now I know why they smell musty, who they are, and why they're here.

The St Bernard—the leader of those obedient, blonde-haired hench-mutts—has appeared on news networks and viral videos spouting dopey save-the-planet catshit. She's the head of the RFAS—Respect For All Species—protest group. They want a world of flower-power pussies who treat all animals the same. They want all species, from horses to hornets to fuckin' *humans*, to live safely, eat a diet of vegetables and fruit, and form closer, kinder relationships.

Madness.

The RFAS are drug-dropping hippies at their best, and violent loons at their worst. And the most terrible thing about being ordered around by this St Bernard?

I used to bone her.

"Poppy," I say, lisping through the pain in my dripping mouth. I spit blood. "I didn't realise you were a fuckin' terrorist."

I broke up with her a few years back, when she asked me to screw her humanstyle: on top, staring into her eyes. But I'm no pervert.

"What the hell are you doing, Buddy?" Poppy asks, aiming her shotgun my way. She has lost weight and, while I hate to admit it, she looks amazing. "This is sick, even for you."

"Sick?" I ask. "It's just sport."

She bears her sharp teeth. "Get your friend to come out, too."

I gesture to Spot to join me. He slinks down the stairs, dejected and scared, and stands at my side. When he glances up at my gory face he looks away quickly, wide-eyed and afraid.

"A poodle?" Poppy asks. She shakes her head. "Look, I only need one of you. So who wants to live?"

Spot doesn't wait a moment. "Me! It was his idea! Let me help you—I'll do anything you say..."

Poppy fires the shotgun. Spot's face caves in, flapping his poodle-curls and showering his chest with blood. He collapses onto his side, dead.

"I can't bear a coward," Poppy says, lowering the gun. "Now where are the rest of these poor, innocent dudes you're forcing to kill each other?"

***

MY MOUTH KEEPS BLEEDING as I ride with my ex-bitch Poppy towards the Breaking Yard. She had given me a clump of paper towels to stuff between my remaining teeth, but I got the impression that it was more to protect the truck's upholstery than out of kindness.

As she drives us through the night away from the massacre at the warehouse, one of her golden retrievers sits beside me with a gun aimed at my chest. I can hear the humans they'd saved from the dudefighting event bumping around in the trailer behind us. I can't tell whether they're communicating with those weird, gibbery sounds they often make, but I assume they are. I shiver.

"Sorry about your friend," Poppy says. "But you know how it is."

"He wasn't my friend. Just a business partner."

But he was, in some ways. When you're used to doing business with the dregs of caninekind, even a twerp like Spot can feel significant. Before he tried to get me killed I felt like I could trust him, and that's more than I can say for most mutts. Now he's gone up to that great kennel in the sky.

"You need to keep better company," Poppy says, guiding the truck through unlit roads, cutting through the gloom with its high beams. She glances at me; a big brooding bitch even after dropping a few pounds. "I have a confession: back when we were dating, I thought I could change you."

I laugh. "What?"

"Yeah. I thought that all you needed to recognise the true way was the love of a good bitch."

And Poppy *did* love good.

I can smell her: the heavy scent of her sex, the sharp pungence of her drool, and the deliciously stale waft of her anal glands. I imagine her wrinkled brow and short muzzle hovering by my asshole, taking a long sniff...

Snap out of it, Buddy.

"'The true way'?" I sneer.

"Love, Buddy," she says. "Love for all, and accepting our place in the world."

Through the darkened windows, I see a signpost: *Bella's Flea Remedies*. But this isn't a factory for killing bloodsucking parasites; this is a compound filled with several dozen humans, captured from the wild or snatched from their owners.

This is the Breaking Yard.

Poppy pulls up the truck with a rattly judder. She looks meaningfully at the golden retriever holding me at gunpoint, leaves the engine running with its blazing headlights lighting up a shadowy copse, then climbs out and slams the door behind her.

"Are you into humans too?" I ask the golden retriever. "Or are you into *her?*"

The golden retriever scowls, the sight of his jagged teeth transforming his elegant features into a deathmask.

"Not much of a talker?" I say.

There's a heavy clunk; the sound of Poppy opening the rear doors. In the mirror, bathed by the red glare of the truck's parking lights, eight humans bound on feet-and-hands out of the trailer. The last one is Pale Yellow, the fat dude with the dented head who Spot had beaten, kept in a cage and trained up, and whose snout I'd swatted before the event. He looks at the truck with a creased face before vanishing into the trees with his companions.

Before Poppy can return, I slam my paw down into the golden retriever's gun. He drops it into the paw-well and I lunge for him, springing my bleeding jaws wide. He barks a call to Poppy, urging her to rush back, but I'm too swift. An alsatian versus a golden retriever might make for a good fight on the street, but he's no match for a seasoned veteran like me. I clamp his neck in my teeth and wrench at it, ignoring the pain in my injured mouth. My growl becomes a gargle as a tsunami of blood washes over my tongue, and when the retriever yips in panic I go in for another chomp, tearing his cheek away with my freshly snapped incisors.

Not so fuckin' pretty now, are you?

The driver's door clicks open behind me and I swing my head around, spraying the windscreen with blood. My ex-lover Poppy leaps onto her seat like a great beast, rocking the vehicle. She's beautiful in her spit-flecked rage, and rams into me with that huge St Bernard weight I'd once found so enticing. My skull crashes against the window as I land on top of the dying golden retriever, and then she's on top of me, a mountain of fur and muscle cloaked in a dense cloud of bitch-stench. Even though she's skinnier than I've ever seen her, I can't match her strength, and my lipstick-prick twitches between my legs as she crushes me. I'm tough, but I don't want to die like this: half-aroused by my own killer.

"Okay, okay," I pant. "I'm done."

"You killed a good dog," she snarls into my ear, plucking the golden retriever's gun from the paw-well and tossing it behind her and out of the vehicle.

"I know."

Poppy's furious face fills my vision. "You don't know anything, Buddy. That's always been the problem."

With her weight constricting my lungs, I gasp, "What?"

"I've seen the future, and we got it wrong. This isn't how things are supposed to be. We should look up to them. We should love them..."

"Submissive catshit," I spit.

Poppy shows her teeth. "Move."

Outside, shots rip through the night: Poppy's hench-mutts clearing the way at the Breaking Yard. Spot and I only ever paid two or three guard dogs to patrol overnight because, we figured, who would want to raid a facility used for training humans to be dudefighters?

Animal rights psychos, that's who.

Shrouded by trees and the satin dark, Poppy holds the scruff of my neck and pokes her shotgun into my ribs, reminding me not to try anything while we wait. Her smell drives me crazy. I have to fight the urge to drop to all fours and start sniffing her, like an animal.

Beyond the noise of exploding guns and ricocheting bullets, I hear something more unsettling: humans. The ones Poppy had set free before we'd left the truck, I assume, babbling into the night, pacing aimlessly over the fields, confused by their sudden freedom. Or are they smarter than that? Are they circling us, with their dumb faces expressionless but a hunger rising in their strange globelike stomachs, but not for food...

Cut it the fuck out.

A howl rises up ahead and Poppy shoves me towards the Breaking Yard.

My guts crawl, unsettled. "Now that you know where this place is, why haven't you killed me?"

From behind, Poppy huffs. "I was going to."

"But then you remembered how good this lipstick is?"

"No," she says. "Then you murdered a hound I trusted. Now I want to show you a better way."

"What does that mean? You're going to make me eat a banana and force me to apologise to these scrotes for making them battle? Give me a break."

"Shut up and keep walking, Buddy."

The Breaking Yard building consists of several smaller rooms, a large chamber filled with rows of connected cages for our trainee combatants, and an outer courtyard at the back. That rear space was for the brutal routines that Spot and our coaches put the humans through to break them, rebuild them, and train them as fighters. In the daytime, the building looks unassuming, but now, in the bullet-torn gloom, it looks foreboding.

The front door has been busted down and Poppy's crew have switched the lights on to illuminate the inner corridor. One of my guard dogs—a pitbull called Rex, if I remember right—lies half-propped by the wall. A fan of splattered blood marks the paintwork behind him and his belly has been shot to shreds, a tumble of viscera spilling from the tattered wound.

"Talking of good dogs," I say. "That guy was raising a family of five, and your mutts slaughtered him."

"If he was working for you, he was a bad boi."

The stink of Rex's half-digested dinner assaults my nose. I look back at her. "The problem with idiots like you, is that you'll choose a peaceful human over a dog."

"And the problem with you, is that you see a problem with that. Keep going."

I step through the gore and move down the passageway. Before I can open the far door, it crashes open and one of Poppy's golden retrievers staggers out, groaning. The miasma of trapped humans fills the corridor and the retriever coughs, tips onto his side, and vomits.

"It's... hell in there..." he groans, his tongue lolling from his teeth.

I turn back to Poppy and the look on her coldly raging face makes me shrink. During the shootout back at the dudefighting event, I was in my element, ready to sneak, hunt, kill, and escape, but the sight of my ex-bitch staring me down causes fear to clasp my bones.

"In," she says. Her voice is blank and empty; inevitable.

I step through the doorway, and the familiar reeking room begins to clatter and scream.

Now, I've been to slaughterhouses before.

I've watched cow skulls get pounded into mush, and seen chicks get shoved into shredding machines. So I've never understood the fuss of doing something similar to a human. So fuckin' what, if they make popular pets? Ducks and rabbits are cute as hell, but they're a lot cuter when they're in my belly.

The Breaking Yard might seem shocking, but that's only because most mutts have a baffling sympathy for humans.

In this room, the trainees are kept in cages stacked double-high, with minimal food and barely enough room to turn around, let alone use a toilet tray. The smell of the piss, shit, filthy human flesh, vomit, blood, and putrefying corpses would turn the stomach of the toughest mutts, but so what? These conditions just mean that the smart humans we were training would work all the harder, to escape their surroundings and make their debut in the fighting pit.

At the far-left corner, we've got 'The Mound'. That's where the exhausted, ruined, or executed humans were piled up and left to rot, and served as a blood-soaked warning for their living pals who might think of rebelling.

Pleasant? No. But am I sorry? Of course not.

"This..." Poppy says, over the caged humans' cacophony, "...is worse than I could have imagined."

Her remaining two golden retrievers stand at either end of the wall of stacked cages, one covering her eyes with a paw, and the other whining to himself and weeping. With Poppy in shock and her dogs crying like pussycats, I could make a break for the door, but the more I think about dying in this place the less I want to.

The noise of shrieking humans and the crashing of metal bars hurts my head, so out of habit I unleash a flurry of stern barks. The animals fall silent but watchful, as if they know that one of their masters has been captured, just like they were.

"Come on then," Poppy says, the menacing vacancy returning to her tone. "Give me the tour."

I jump when she lifts her shotgun and pumps the rack.

"Fine. Well. This is where we keep them. Obviously."

"And where do they use the bathroom?"

"They're *humans.* They don't care about where they go..."

"Actually they do," she says, her voice monotone but her eyes like wells of sorrow. "Humans are clean animals, in the wild."

"They go in their cages, or whenever we let them out."

"And what is that?" she asks, nodding towards the corpses.

"That's The Mound," I say. "They sometimes stop eating, or try to bite one of the trainers."

"So you kill them and put them on display."

I stare at the hillock of flesh, where the only motion is the crawling and flitting of flies. The fresher bodies are coloured from the lightest pale to the deepest dark, and the blue of their blood contrasts with the range of their mouldering skin tones. The closest human to us lies on her back with her legs propped up on the mountain of bodies, eyes staring and skull broken.

"Yes, we leave them for the others to see," I say. "Look, it's just business, Poppy..."

"Where do you train them to fight?"

I sigh and lead her to the door by the furthest cage. The bearded human trapped inside gazes vacantly up at me. "Through here."

I flick a switch on the wall and we head outside.

In the cold glow of the Breaking Yard floodlights, for a moment I wonder if we really did go too far. The carnage out here makes The Mound look like a solemn, respectful burial place.

Strips of heavy or sharpened metal litter the naked soil. Wherever the ground isn't layered with steel weaponry, it bears scraps of flesh, sliced limbs, hacked torsos and severed human heads. At my feet, a slashed penis lies deflated and puny in a dried pool of blood; to its side, the smeared cleaver I had watched cut the organ free; beside that, the human that had once wielded the blade, its jaw torn completely off and its head reduced to a nest of shattered bone and glooped brain.

The glazed eyes of a hundred or more carcasses point up towards the stars, twinkling in the glow of the flood lamps. A frayed carpet of cadavers. A morbid human blanket.

In the quietest voice I've ever heard her speak, Poppy asks, "How are there so many?"

I shrug. "We wanted to find the best. Most of them weren't up to it."

Without a word, she returns to the door.

The Breaking Yard is cordoned off by brick walls topped with razor wire, so I've nothing to do except follow her back inside.

Poppy surveys the cages, rubbing her chin with her paw, then approaches a cell containing a lithe younger human with a beard. "You need to learn why what you did was so wrong," Poppy says. "You need to understand."

The other two dogs have pulled themselves together. One blocks the entrance, and the other looms behind me by the door leading out to the training grounds. Both aim their pistols my way.

Poppy reaches through the bars and the bearded human sniffs her paw. Just as I think he's going to bite her, he rubs his face against her pad. "Haven't you ever felt the pull of your true self?"

Hippy catshit, I think.

"Don't you think there's a chance that we got things wrong? That maybe, just maybe, humans and dogs should interact differently? More closely?"

Unbidden, something stirs in my mind.

"Unlock its cage," Poppy says.

I gaze at the enclosures and along the line of human eyes pointing my way. A chill of hatred slips across my fur.

Is it hatred, though? I wonder, as I go to the wall-mounted electronic keypad and press the 'Unlock' button for cage number 7. The cage emits a solid clank. Its door swings open. *Is it hatred, or...*

"You're scared of them, Buddy," Poppy says, peering into the younger one's open cage. "But you don't need to be. They want to help us."

"'Help us'," I scoff, but my knees have grown weak.

"Yes," she says, pulling the human by its flank and encouraging it to leave its confinement.

Dread fills me as this bitch, *my ex-bitch*, crouches down beside the human and strokes her hairy paw across its spine, down its rear, and then back up to its chest.

"Poppy..." I say.

The golden retrievers jab the air with their guns, reminding me that I've nowhere to go. I don't want to die here, in this stinking place, and I don't want to see whatever Poppy wants to show me.

The human responds to her touch as she tugs it up towards her, dragging its front limbs off the ground.

"These humans are so much smarter than you realise, Buddy. They can help us. They deserve our respect."

Poppy heaves and the wretched creature grunts, its back limbs straining and shaking with effort.

"This is the way, Buddy," she says, gazing at the human as it struggles to stay upright. "The true way."

My head spins, the room sways, and my eyes rebel against the monstrous sight. This vile degenerate was once mine, and now she wants to show me... what? That humans are somehow just as good, or even *better* than us? It's wrong and I need to leave, because I don't want to be sick or faint or just drop dead on the spot.

The human pants, wobbling on its back limbs as Poppy releases him.

It stands.

The golden retrievers are distracted by the grotesque spectacle, so in a final act of desperation I press the big red button on the keypad that reads 'Unlock All'.

There's a series of metallic clangs as each of the cage doors bursts open.

"No!" Poppy howls. "Not all at once!"

The freed humans clamber screaming from their confines, and without thinking I drop to all fours and dash for the door. It feels almost natural, sprinting on four legs instead of two, and despite the two golden retrievers firing off a couple of shots there's no pain or wounds as I rush past one into the passageway.

The room behind swells with those incomprehensible human squeals, and a flurry of barks and yet more gunshots follow—but me? I'm free. I'm down on all four paws and bolting from the Breaking Yard like a rocket into the night.

Outside, the moon and stars fill the sky and the trees beyond ring with the strange hoots and jabbering of the humans—those Poppy had freed from the truck, and perhaps more besides. With my heart pounding in my head and against my ribs, I run blindly through tall grass and scraping tree branches. There's joy in my chest as I make my escape, and an odd kind of freedom in moving closer to the ground than I've ever moved before, like a beast, or even like a human. It's wrong but it's liberating.

I will sprint all the way back to my kennel in the city, and end this terrible day with a bowl of beer and a plate of jellied ox. I'll relax, curled up in my bed, and never even consider another racket involving humans again. Poppy may have been right when she said we had gone too far with the dudefighting event. Maybe things *do* need to change between dogs and humans, but not the way she wants. Not like...

In the shadowed forest, something grabs my throat.

I whimper and strain but I'm exhausted, and whatever holds me tightens its grip. It's not a paw or even a hand; it's a leash.

A silhouette moves amidst the black; a tall figure with a dented lump for a head. It's Pale Yellow, the human from the dudefighting event, and it's standing upright on two legs.

Pale Yellow reaches down and pets my head, and I'm too

tired to fight back. More smells assail me as I notice a crowd of them, surrounding me as I crouch alone and temporarily tamed in these woods, with a collar around my neck and a human I'd once beaten standing straight and stroking the hair on my skull.

An urge awakens in me which reaches way back into history, to a time when neither humans nor dogs ruled the world, and the outcome of our twin evolutionary race remained unclaimed.

The feeling is somehow both comforting and terrifying.

My tail begins to wag.

Jonathan Butcher is an English writer who likes to tell strange, unique, and usually dark tales. When he was 7 years old, his teacher banned him from writing about ghosts or monsters for an entire term - but he hasn't stopped since.

HOUSEWARMING

MICHELLE VON ESCHEN

There's a lot to learn about a house you've only just purchased, things they don't mention on the listing, quirks and oddities intentionally left out of the bullet list. Impossible to quantify on assignment, they are the things one only discovers after time spent living there. Some of them are good, lovely surprises, like the way the light travels through the living room in the springtime––the April rays painting rainbows on the walls––and how generations of Mallard ducks have flown into the backyard year after year to have their babies, a guaranteed gaggle of recipients for the torn-up bread of many loaves gone stale.

Most of the revelations are not worth the purchase price however, like the one window that rattles every windstorm and can't be replaced without a costly hassle due to its odd size, how miserably hot the converted attic gets in the summer, and the imperceptible slope in the garden that threatens to flood the ground floor every time it rains.

And where the listing failed to mention them, the showing

continues the deception, expertly scheduled by the agents for a calm, clear day with no threat of wind or showers.

When you buy a house, you slowly and simultaneously fall in love and out of it as those million tiny inheritances are, through time and proximity, disclosed.

We spent the early morning moving into the "two-story with basement," hauling load after load of things we couldn't bear to leave behind, the front door propped open like a yawning mouth commensurate with our growing exhaustion. I heft a box of our belongings onto a small stack in the entry.

"That's the last one!" I call to my husband, Rhett. I hear him sliding things across the countertop in the kitchen and I peek my head in. "Hon?"

"Oh thank God." He wipes his brow and begins to cough. It starts small, but with each hack it grows until he's bent over the counter, near expelling a lung. The fit is suggestive, causing a tickle to hit my throat and for me to join him.

"Man, these coughs need to go," I say when I finally clear it.

"I really think it's the stress of the move, Lora."

He begins to open one of the boxes, but I reach out a hand to stop him. "Then that can wait. Catch your breath. We did it!"

"We *did* do it."

"Now, can you *believe* all this cabinet space!" I open every door like a child seeking something hidden, yanking handle after handle to expose every inch of gaudy adhesive shelf liner. From one of the shelves above the fridge, an orange plastic pet food bowl falls to the ground and spins briefly like a top before settling right-side-up on the tile. A moment later, a shadow passes by the kitchen doorway, accompanied by a sound like rain hitting a metal rooftop. I follow the noise to the back door where I find a dog, its overgrown nails clattering as it scrambles on the slick wood floor of the hallway. The golden retriever with a pale orange coat whines when it sees me.

"It's okay." I step closer.

The dog whines more and begins to bark before lowering itself into a submissive crouch. Panting, either from excitement, exhaustion or some combination, it rolls over and presents its belly. I take its new position as an invite and kneel down to rub its belly. Whatever spot I find does the trick and soon its breath is soft and content aside from an occasional wheeze.

"It's a boy!" Rhett exclaims like he's announcing the gender of a child.

When the dog sees Rhett, he whines again and thumps his tail hard on the floor.

Rhett points to the dog's neck. "He's wearing a collar. Check for a tag."

"Hi sweetheart," I say as I move closer to his head. The dog sneezes and a long string of snot shoots from a nostril, dangling and swinging back and forth, a pendulum of frothy, discolored mucus nearly keeping the time.

"Ugh. He's got a cold or something."

The snot disappears back into his nose on the next inhale, clearing a path for me to present a hand slowly for inspection. The dog gives it a good sniff. I pet his head, then his neck until I can tug the collar, revealing the small, circular tag hanging from it. Engraved into one side of the metal is the name *Biscuit*.

"Where do you live, Biscuit?" I ask. His ears perk up at the mention of his name. I flip the medallion and see an address I'm only beginning to recognize as our own.

Rhett leans in. "Is it somewhere close?"

"You could say that."

"Well?"

"It says he lives here. The agent didn't mention a dog."

"No, she didn't, but he could have lived here before us! I read about a dog that ran off at a rest stop when a family was moving out of state. He walked all the way back to his old house."

"Did you have a long journey, Biscuit?" I ask as I carefully inspect his paws, which are reddened and raw in some spots.

Rhett smiles. "His family will come looking for him here if that's the case. Guess we'll just have to keep him while we wait, let his paws heal."

"I don't know. We just got here, we don't have any dog food, and did you forget about my allergies?"

"We've got allergy tablets in one of the bathroom boxes, dogs will eat anything, and technically we are guests in *his* house."

"You've got an answer for everything."

"Come on, Lo, you love me for it."

"Ask me if I do when I'm covered in hives."

"Don't be so dramatic. It's a mild allergy at its worst. I'll find something for him to eat."

While Rhett scours the kitchen stacks I search the towers of boxes in the living room for the contents of our old medicine cabinet.

"Allergy tablets for me and some Neosporin for you, Biscuit."

I dry swallow the pills and sit on the floor to call him over to me. With coaxing, I manage to get him lying on his back again, a position which enables me to apply a thin layer of the healing ointment to the circular patches of raw flesh on his pads.

Suddenly, Biscuit hears something in dog decibels that compels him to pull away and career onto the newly placed couch to give a retaliatory bark through the living room window. I stand up and follow his gaze to the sidewalk, where a woman stands, looking in our direction. The brunette eyes the front garden and then the house.

"It's okay. It's just a neighbor."

I raise a hand to wave, but the woman only takes a flyer from the For Sale sign and walks back to a waiting car, paying neither Biscuit nor I any attention. I run to the front door and out onto the stoop, where Biscuit flies by me and toward the car, barking his head off at the perceived invader.

"It's not for sale anymore!" I try to yell over his woofs, but she's already pulled closed the passenger side door. I join Biscuit at the curb and yank the remaining flyers from the plastic holder. Biscuit watches eagerly as I throw them in the recycling. I stop and smell the air, which feels thick with humidity.

"Come on, boy, let's get back inside."

I shut the front door with more force than necessary and the windows tremble from the shockwave.

"What's all the noise about?" Rhett asks from the kitchen door, the orange pet food bowl in his hands.

"I don't know why the agency hasn't put the SOLD sign up. It's confusing people."

"The agents know we're here. If anyone calls for a showing, they'll let them know the house isn't available anymore."

"Yeah, I guess."

Rhett tilts the pet food bowl to Biscuit's nose to lead him into the kitchen. He sets the bowl on the floor. "Eat up, boy! First and last time you're getting canned tuna as a meal."

Biscuit wolfs down the fish with greed while wagging his tail. He seems grateful for the snack until he begins to retch. Rhett and I panic in a weirdly synchronized dance around the dog.

"He's going to barf!" I scream.

"Keep him in the kitchen, Lora!" Rhett bellows back.

Only moments later, the three of us stand above a slimy pile of tuna and black chunks as it steams on the linoleum. I don't want to look closer at it, but flecks of red dot the surface.

"Is that blood?"

Holding his nose, Rhett leans closer. "He probably ate all sorts of garbage on his way back to the house. Wouldn't take much to make his stomach unhappy."

Before I can stop him, Biscuit licks up the mess and trots without care back to the living room.

Rhett grabs his tool bag and gives me a peck on the cheek. "Before I can think anymore about what I just saw, I'm going to take some of my tools down to the basement and scope it out."

"Future man cave daydreams?"

"Not too distant. I've already got some plans."

"Okay, but you can't start any new projects until we get everything unpacked. Deal?"

He kisses me again, this time on my forehead, a show of affection that makes me feel safe.

"Deal."

Throughout the morning, I unpack boxes as I need things. One in the living room when I need a power strip, which sparks wildly when I plug it in, one in the bathroom for toilet paper rolls, which are soggy and bloated to twice their size, and one in the kitchen for a cup, but its plastic is twisted and misshapen as though it melted in the move. I check the other plastic kitchenware and none of it looks as it did before the long journey here. The salad spinner has collapsed in on itself and the lid has fused to the bowl, the large pasta strainer's holes have all closed up, and the dry measuring cup set is now one tangled ball of multi-colored plastic. Over the course of those hours, the house should feel more like a home, but nothing feels right at all. Everything this end of the move seems worse for the wear.

Rhett emerges from the basement, fresh from planning his dude den, and surveys the cardboard and newspaper mess.

"Babe, the house looks great! I can't believe how much you've gotten done."

His excitement fades when he sees the disappointment on my face.

"What's wrong?"

"The devil is in the details."

"Huh?"

I show him the damaged items. "We have to replace so much."

"No move goes without its hitches. Remember when we rented that apartment and the moving company mixed up our stuff with another family's? That was much worse than a few warped cups. I bet the van got too warm in this weather. There's no insulation in those things."

"There's more. Look at my hands." I hold them up for him to inspect. A black dusting shadows my skin, collecting in the minute crevasses of my palm prints. "It's like everything went into the boxes dirty."

He drags a finger across one of my palms, leaving a trail in the residue. "The house feels a little humid, maybe it's pulling the ink from the newspaper we used as wrapping?"

"We didn't wrap the couch and it's grimy too. I don't get it."

"Have you unpacked the cleaning stuff? There's a tub of wipes somewhere." He spends a few minutes rummaging without direction. The dog comes to investigate, mistaking the shuffling for treats. My husband pets him and pulls his hand away from Biscuit's fur. "Ugh, whatever it is, it's all over the dog too."

"It might be easier to pick some cleaner up in town. I can go."

"No, no. We've done enough running around. It can wait."

"How's the basement?"

"There's some pooled water in a couple spots, but I can't see any cracks in the foundation. Next time it rains, I'll find out how it's getting in."

"Pooled water? Did we make the right decision?"

"Oh babe, don't start. You know this will be a good change." He finds a roll of garbage bags, pulls a single one from the group, and lays it down on the couch with a flourish of his hand. "Madam, your seat."

I take the improvised throne and Biscuit jumps up to crawl into my lap, eager for more love now that my hands aren't busy unpacking. In no time he's out and I allow myself to catch a quick nap too.

When I wake, a rash covers my forearms where Biscuit was resting on them. He wheezes and his reddened eyes water. "Poor thing. Looks like we're allergic to each other."

The afternoon sun shines through the living room window, projecting a golden ray onto the far corner of the room. Rhett is there with his back to me, hands on his hips as he stares at the wallpaper, a chaotic meadow motif of infinite colors.

"How was your nap?" he asks without looking in my direction.

"What are you doing?" I shift on the couch and Biscuit sneezes another impossibly long string of snot from his nose.

"Just watch."

"Wha-"

"There!" He points at a high spot of the corner where a strip of the wallpaper performs acrobatics as it leaps from the wall, tucking and rolling into itself like the shedding skin of a Paper-bark Maple. "Third time it's done that."

I shoo the snotty dog off of me to join Rhett in the corner and run a hand up the wall, smoothing out the paper against its curl, but it resists any tack and dives once more.

"It's not sticking at all."

"Shoddy work probably. A lot of those house flippers don't

know when to call in the experts. They opt for cost savings over quality."

Another strip releases itself and heads toward the floor. "I think the walls are rejecting this ugly paper and I don't blame them."

"The good news is, Lo, the house is *ours* now and we get to do whatever we want. You want to tear off the rest of this ugly wallpaper? I'm all for it. *Fuck* chaotic meadows."

"Fuck 'em," I say, as I pull a strip from the wall.

"That's the spirit! Don't stop now!" Rhett plays *We Are the Champions* on the Bluetooth speaker and we take turns ripping the failing wallpaper down.

When I've shredded enough meadow, I check my phone, hoping one of my friends has messaged a *Good luck with the move!* or a *how is it going?*, but the notification screen is empty.

"Don't look so sad, babe," Rhett says, "we're in the middle of a move. People know we're busy. Send a message so they know it's okay to reply."

The house is great, I type in the group chat, *and get this, a dog just showed up out of nowhere, walked right in!*

The message tries to send, but I know it's futile when I see I have no bars. "That's annoying."

"Hmm?"

"Cell service is shit here. The message won't send."

"Maybe they *have* messaged you then and the messages just haven't come through yet. We'll get everything sorted with plenty of time to plan the housewarming party, don't worry."

"There's so much to do," I say through a yawn as I check my phone again. "God, it's 6:30! How long did I nap?"

"Doesn't matter. You needed it and you're *still* tired."

"There's no rule against an early bedtime."

"We can eat and fall asleep watching something?"

"I'd love that."

Rhett and I unwrap the television from its bubble wrap cocoon, which thankfully protected the screen in the move. I find the remotes while he heats a frozen mac and cheese in the microwave for us to share. Like a dream, the warm food and a half hour of cuddling in front of *Fixer Upper* weighs down my eyelids. Though I'm tired, I feel empowered. If Chip and Joanna can work miracles, why can't we?

"Time for bed then?" Rhett asks, noticing my battle to stay awake, though he's looking at Biscuit as he says it.

"Before you ask, no he *cannot* sleep with us. The allergy med is nothing against this rash. It's already getting worse."

"You were scratching it in your sleep, Lo."

"Sure, but I wouldn't have it to begin with if he wasn't attached to me like a shadow. We'll have to put something together for him down here."

Rhett layers broken-down cardboard boxes into a thick stack near the back door and covers it with a couple of quilts.

"Here ya go, boy."

Biscuit whines and refuses to step on the ramshackle bed.

"It's not that bad!"

Rhett picks him up and sets him down on top of the quilts, but Biscuit steps off and runs upstairs.

"Ugh. This is why you don't have kids or dogs. They just take too much effort."

"I don't know what you want me to do, hon? He wants to sleep with us. How are you going to tell him no?"

"Bring the bed you built upstairs. He can sleep on the floor in front of our bed, but that's as close as he's getting if you like me having skin on my arms."

We head upstairs to our own bed which isn't much more glamorous than Biscuit's, it being only a sheeted mattress on the floor. I dig out my favorite pair of pajama pants from the travel luggage we used to move our clothes. As I pull them on, one of my fingers snags in a hole near the waist band. I hold them up to the light of the table lamp on the floor.

"Are you kidding me? They've got holes in them! They look moth-eaten."

"Guess you'll have to go commando with me!" Rhett grins from his spot on the bed.

I drop my hands to my sides. "How can you be so positive? Almost nothing has gone right today."

"That's just life, though, isn't it? No use adding to the shit with a bad attitude."

I lay down beside him and turn out the lamp. "Night, Rhett."

"Goodnight, babe. I love you. Welcome home."

I don't tell him I love him back; instead, I stew in the dark, listening to Biscuit slowly creep closer until I can feel his paws touching my leg.

Hours pass while I toss and turn, my mind unable to stop reviewing the strangeness of the day.

"Rhett?" I ask once, but he doesn't stir. "Rhett!" I call, closer to his head.

He turns over and his weight pulls me closer. "What?"

"Something is wrong with the house."

He shifts again and there's frustration in the movement. "You say that every time we move. The last house had too many cracks in the walls. You thought the ceiling was going to collapse. The one before that had too many bugs. What is it now? What's wrong with this one?"

"This is different, I think. On a fundamental level."

"The foundation is solid, remember? No cracks."

"Not foundational, *fundamental*. There's something not right here."

"We've been here one day. I bet you in a week you'll be in love with the place."

"No, I don't think I will. The wallpaper, the dirt, the water in the basement, the dog..." I touch my forearms, where the strange rash has spread in both directions, to my elbows and wrists. "This rash. It's a lot for one day."

"It's always *something*. What will it be tomorrow?"

"You've been supportive all day and now you're turning on me. I'm right about this and the dog feels the same way."

"That it's always something with you?"

I can't help but laugh. His joke breaks the tension enough for us to hold each other until another joint coughing fit forces us apart.

Rhett falls back to sleep quickly and I continue to lie awake, painfully aware of the foreign creaks and groans of our new abode and the increasing discomfort of my arms. *The ceiling isn't collapsing. The bugs aren't taking over.*

Sometime around one in the morning, my fear of noises is replaced by something awful I smell.

"Do you smell that?" I ask Rhett while shaking him awake, wasting no time whispering to rouse him.

"Hmm?" He rolls over in the dark.

"It smells like smoke."

He's silent for a moment, like improved hearing will increase his chances of picking up the smell, but then he jumps out of bed and flicks on the light without warning, temporarily blinding my dark-adjusted eyes. I can't get mad, it's the reaction I need him to have. He can be so dismissive, but smoke is serious and he's taking it that way.

We search the house and Biscuit follows, sniffing the air and whimpering.

I inhale all the corners of the living room, drag my nostrils along the vertical planes of the walls, now pinstriped in missing sheets of wallpaper. "It's coming from in here."

"I don't know, I smell it in here," Rhett calls from the dining room.

In the kitchen, I walk through pockets of invisible smoke. "It's everywhere."

"I checked the detectors earlier. They've all got new batteries. We should be hearing alarms."

I peer out the living room window into the growing dawn. Nothing burns outside, no neighbors fill the streets watching a blaze. "Should we open some windows?"

"I don't smell it anymore. Do you?"

"No. It's gone. That's weird."

"It must have blown in from one of the farms nearby. They do those big burn piles."

"Yeah, that's probably it."

We head back to bed and despite or maybe because of the trauma of smelling smoke, I'm exhausted and can't fight sleep any longer.

In the morning, I wake up to Biscuit's fur in my face and move it to see he has straddled both Rhett and I in the night. My face itches and my throat has begun to tighten. I should be cold, having slept nude, but I'm sweating and I can see bubbles of perspiration pop from Rhett's forehead. Maybe we're sick. Maybe the coughing was the beginning of something.

I move Biscuit, who steals my side of the bed as I wrap myself in a robe and head downstairs. Halfway down the steps, the front door unlocks and pushes inward. I run back to my sleeping husband.

"Rhett," I hiss. "There's someone in the house!"

He wakes with a shudder. "What the fuck?"

I shush him to whisper and it sets off a coughing fit that I try to stifle. The last thing I need is for the intruder to know we're here.

"Maybe they thought the house was empty?"

"They have keys!"

He finds his own robe and heads to the top of the stairs to investigate. Biscuit and I follow.

"They've done a great job of renovating the place." The voice is feminine and authoritative, but familiar. It's our real estate agent, Kenna Massen. "Isn't it nice?"

Two other voices mutter in agreement.

Kenna continues, "Hard to believe it almost burned down."

"It almost what? Did you hear that, Rhett?"

Rhett turns to me and his mouth hangs open, but he doesn't reply.

"Why the fuck has she brought people to look at our house? That's not normal, is it?"

"I don't think so," he manages.

"And I told you, Rhett! There *is* something wrong with the house! Why didn't she tell us it had structural damage?"

"I don't know, Lora! They don't have to disclose that type of thing? We didn't ask?"

I shift my focus back to the conversation downstairs.

"All from a faulty extension cord," Kenna explains. "This whole place was filled with smoke. They had to hose it down. Now there are a couple puddles in the basement that still need to dry out and the wallpaper will need redoing, as you can see."

"Everything makes sense now!" I whisper to Rhett.

"I'm a DIY freak so I'm ready for the work," a woman chimes. "And the price is unbeatable."

"The death discount," a man says.

"Honey!" the DIY freak snaps.

"Died?" A warmth spreads from my cheeks to my neck.

"How many died? It doesn't put us off the place."

"No, no one died! Just some damage that's all cleaned up now!"

"We did some Googling. We saw the news stories. You don't have to lie," the man explains.

"Forgive my husban-" the woman starts.

"It used to be that you had maybe fifteen minutes to escape a burning house." Kenna's voice sounds distant, like she can see the flames.

I smell smoke again and something else.

"But with all the synthetic materials surrounding us these days, that window of safety is only about three minutes."

I smell burning hair.

I look to Rhett for help and he begins to wiggle in my vision, a mirage of life, a dissipating oasis.

"They were asleep when it started."

His hair smolders and the skin beneath shrinks and pulls away to nothing, revealing his skull.

"Oh my god!" I scream, with a voice growing hoarser by the moment. A searing ache pulses through my marrow.

"They were a lovely couple. I sold them this house."

The rash on my arm changes color from red to black, a lava field of flame and soot.

"They had a dog. You know, it was the dog who tried to save them. He barked to wake them, according to the neighbors, but it was too late."

The words hit me like bricks. "Biscuit was ours. He tried to save us," I tell Rhett, but Rhett is char and ember, liquefying the carpet beneath him to form a soup of him and house. His eye sockets are wide with surprise, but empty. His eyeballs have already melted and dripped down his cheekbones like tears. I cough smoke.

"What's happening?" Holes open in my chest and arms and face. I feel the cool morning air on my rear molars.

"The smoke and the fire had already found them," Kenna adds.

"That's terrible," the man says.

"And the dog?" the woman asks.

I look at Biscuit on the stairs, quiet until now. He barks at Rhett and I as we die all over again in front of him. I bring a finger, its tip covered in blisters filled to bursting, to my lips to shush him.

"Did you hear that?" Kenna sounds scared.

"It sounded like a dog." The woman sounds just as frightened.

I watch the man come to the bottom of the stairwell. "Oh, you poor thing!" he says to Biscuit, who cowers and whimpers and barks. "How'd you get in here?"

Kenna comes to stand next to the man. "My god, that's him! That's their dog!"

The woman begins to cry. "He survived and he's looking for them!"

Rhett and I begin to blow away as the central air kicks in, sending bits of us to settle on everything.

Kenna tuts and sighs. "What a good dog. Loyal even after their end."

Michelle von Eschen (early works written as Michelle Kilmer) is an American author of quiet, literary horror and dark, speculative fiction. She is a lover of the macabre who prefers Earl Grey tea, October, people who say goodbye on the phone, and her dreams are so real she can't figure out what has really happened to her. When she isn't writing, Michelle enjoys the outdoors, weightlifting, dark beer, web design, singing and playing guitar, and watching horror movies. She lives in England with her husband, horror author Jonathan Butcher.

THE BOY WHO RAN WITH DOGS

RJ BENETTI

Husband beats wife. Wife beats Husband. They beat each other. They both beat the boy. Inside isn't safe. It's dimly lit and chilling and without kindness. Nothing is kind. Not now.

Nor was it ever for the boy.

They hit him again.

"Why do you smell like baby shit?"

"Why are you so dumb?"

"You're just like your drunk father!"

"You're a fucking whore like your mother!"

"What are you, a fairy?"

SMACK. SMACK. SMACK.

It's not safe. Everything smells like blood.

Night takes over.

The boy travels the streets of the city, his face welted above a purple-spotted body. His lips punched bloody, crusting crimson.

He huddles within himself, breathing shuddered, knees to chest in the grey, monochrome alleyway.

The cold's getting into his bones.

Garbage stench sears his nostrils.

The dumpster he leans against is blue and big, towering over him. The boy who doesn't even know his name. The boy who hasn't been to school. The boy who never knew *true* parents.

And he hears growling. He raises his head while his ears prick.

Snarls. Bites. Barks. Whimpers.

Violence. It's here too. And it's close. Panic sets in. He can't get away.

RUFF-RUFF-RUFF! More biting. Crying. Whimpering.

Something dying.

He understands.

The boy stands, knees wobbling, nearly rapping against each other like billiard balls. He shambles forth, a small and rakish shadow, investigating with his little heart in his throat.

A pit bull is on top of a wiry-haired terrier, one-third its size. Teeth sinking into its back; it whips its head. The terrier squeals, blood spraying.

It's helpless.

NO!

Looking to the dumpster, he sees an empty wine bottle, tilted askew upon a mound of rot. Without thinking, he snatches it. And he bounds forth. Until-

The bottle shatters over the pit bull's head.

CRACK.

Then he stabs the animal. Jabbing the broken vessel through its white fur, slicing the elastic fascia of its dense hide, up and down its body, then up and down again. *Squelch. Squelch. Squelch.*

The pit won't let go. The dog's still crying. Still helpless. Just like the boy. He can relate. A white ball of anger swells in his chest.

He feels a connection.

He feels *oneness.*

The half-bottle sinks deep into the pit bull's neck, serrating through the coiled muscle. The terrier falls as its jaws loosen. The pit's growling and barking up blood and the boy's shimmying the bottle deeper, working it back and forth until it scrapes vertebrae then punctures the esophageal tube.

Vascular aggression unfurls itself, loosens and goes slack while the knees bend in and the big dog's melon clacks against cement.

Its tongue lolls from its mouth, sidewise like a wet ribbon, blood-dripped, all twitching.

The boy drops the bottle—then drops to his knees to console the terrier.

Weeping, he scoops it in his arms. The dog's a quivering thing, bleary eyes bulging and bulbous, panting in its fret. Other than the gushing blood, he's much the same.

Much the same.

With spirits interweaving, the two remain in the alley, rocking, feeling the forming of the pack.

THE RAT TERRIER TERRORIZES RATS.

Snuffing them out, snatching them from the busy, somber, arterial network of city streets. All healed but with a lumpy back, deformed by way of scar tissue. She brings the rodents to the boy.

The boy sits in a maze of cardboard boxes, a litter of puppies at his back. Whining, eyes mere trembling lines. He'd saved her, which meant he'd saved her unborn too.

When he did it, when he killed the strong pit, he didn't know her womb held life.

But after he found out.

He was glad that it did.

Two Years Later

Moving into the woods of New Jersey, the pack grew in number. First, it was only the terrier, the boy, and her seven living progeny. Three had gone to the other side.

One as a pup,

too weak to breathe.

One as a six-monther,

pulped by a bus.

One simply ran off after a cat,

never to be seen again.

They collected more strays. Like a snowball, expanding with snarling, feral intention. The pack developed; their hierarchy evolved. The boy stayed at the top, ruling over mongrel Dobermans, huskies, rottweilers, chihuahuas, and labs.

All mutts. He could see it in their faces.

He could see it in their snouts.

They had no home and their only identity was instinct.

He was much the same.

THE BOY CALLS HIMSELF *BUMF!* He makes a cheek-coughing, snuffing sound when he does it, thumbing his chest while looking into his brethren's eyes.

They understand. Even though they, themselves, don't have names.

The rat terrier gets special noises from *Bumf!* A squeaky, cooing rendition when he pets her. The others are just grunts. Kind grunts often.

Directive grunts others.

They listen to their alpha.

He's proved himself.

He's spilled blood.

Months Prior

The pack moves through the shadows of the city. They slink around the yellow halos of the street lamps. They skulk only in the darkness.

Ill intent oiling their joints.

Of the city humans, only a few are awake.

One a half-slumbering, wet-brained wino.

A dipsomaniac sex offender, spitting through his gums, cursing his bad luck. His face is peppered with forlorn hairs.

Bumf! makes some hand signals, his arms dancing, bending, flicking forward in the dark obscurity. His dogs, led by the rat terrier, bow their heads in unison before loping forward.

Burping, preoccupied with the bubbly bile in his throat, the wino doesn't see them coming. Doesn't even notice until that last moment, when fur meets flesh, when the incisors of a mangy German Shepherd chomp through the muscles on the side of his neck.

He falls to the side, shock bulging his eyes, blood spouting, piss sopping his crotch, while the rat terrier chews off his bulbous, vessel-netted nose.

Growling, snapping, they sup, they chew, they move aside. The boy, now *Bumf!*, kneels beside the mangled heap of a bum. He dips his fingers into his warm corpse, burrowing them deep into the chest, feeling the sharp pieces, and the wet, sloppy ones before he grabs the heart.

It beats.

Barely.

But it beats.

Then he wrenches it free, feeling arteries *pop* while smelling human copper mist the air. The heart's brought to his toothy mouth, the boy bites down, impatient, unthinking, thriving only on instinct.

Feeling the heart fill his mouth.

Feeling the quivering muscle slide down his throat.

Filling his insides.

He barely chews. After a few more bites, after tearing additional swathes of cardiac tissue free, he tosses the rest of the heart to his pack. They fall upon it with eager snouts.

Masticating with abandon.

With ravenous, wild, abandon.

HE SMEARED the blood on his face. The bum blood. The vagrant's fluid. Inside and now out. It smells like the man's life. It smells like liquor.

Like poisoned inebriants.

A vice metastasized.

They arrive at the boy's old stoop. Before he became *Bumf!* And the boy fishes around in an empty plant potter, bringing forth a key.

Soon, the door swings open and they're inside, a pack of creatures swarming around the boy before fanning out, moving into the dank living room.

His father is asleep, a beer spilling in his lap as he lounges and stutters snores from his recliner. A single bite, jaws wrapping around his naked foot, and after a *crunch*, he's awake.

"AHHHH!"

The Doberman-lab leaps onto his chest, begins gnawing into the dewy flesh of his unwashed face. Tearing his five o' clock shadow away.

Gore flooding, his face is left a dazed red skull, slippery tendons exposed beneath popping scared eyes.

"You!" the man garbles.

Before the rest of the pack falls upon him, teeth rending, paws flashing, the boy is with them, chewing, but not for sustenance, biting in the name of hateful instinct.

The fetor of death and feces fills the dim room. His mom is next, bounding around the corner, then shrilling from her throat.

This time, the boy is first to bite.

Years Later

He grows. The forests of New Jersey are inhospitable. Bleak in their unforgiving darkness, mere patches of arboreal nature struggling to survive in the undeveloped areas between budding cityscapes, abutting sprawling projects, and uneven roads.

The boy is sixteen now and the only language he knows is canine bred. The bristling of backs. Throaty growls. The licking. The never-ending licking. The hunkering down with others for warmth.

The sharing of scraps from dumpsters.

They move out like they always do, the rat terrier now slowed and limping, with cancer eating its spine.

A whimper is exhaled with every patter over crumbling asphalt. The noise hurts the boy. Pangs *Bumf!*

She's the only mother he's ever known.

Up ahead, a gas station glows neon, the bright blues and greens visible through the creaking boughs of a black walnut tree. And there's the dumpster, similar to the one that started it all, only onyx in its coloring.

They skulk across the street in their collective scavenger prowl, innumerable paws padding as they draw near.

They arrive.

***

FLIPPING THE LID OPEN, *Bumf!* is pleased to see mounds of discarded food. Sandwiches, taco meat, burgers. He jumps in while the others keep a prowling watch. And he reaches, until-

"AH!"

Claws rake the back of his grabbing hand, pulling red troughs through the flesh. *Bumf!* recoils, falling back into the trash.

And a figure starts to rise. As the silhouette materializes, just a slender, tenebrous creature hatched from the amorphous refuse, *Bumf!* begins grunting to his pack

His heart flips as they bark outside the dumpster; his nerves rattle then twist as some begin to howl; a coarse lump forms in his throat as he hears his rat terrier mother, mewling, shrilling.

Trash falls from the now hissing figure. Cluttered napkins and hot dog wrappers, cigarette packs and soiled receipts. She's baring her teeth... her, *human* teeth, and *Bumf!* can see her now, in all her demented, backwards grandeur.

Filthy hair shorn inches high—disheveled as if done with scissors, without the presence of a mirror or the guidance of trusted hands. She wears her nails long and pointed, and they're curling now as they dawdle on the crooked, reedy arms before her.

The clothing of the girl is much like *Bumf!'s*, rags and tattered canvas held together by weeping gossamers. Only her attire hangs loose on a slim, feminine, and obviously lithe frame.

Obvious, because of the way she moves forth.

Or bounds, rather.

Leaping on top of the boy who runs with dogs, slashing at him while biting into his protesting hand.

He fights back, flinging her off, hearing that metallic *ping* as her spine bounces off the dumpster's interior. As he leaps onto her, biting and re-ripping her clothes, he hearkens to some commotion outside.

His dogs have ceased barking. Now, they growl. He raises his head while his ears prick.

Snarls. Bites. Barks. Whimpers.

More violence. It's outside too. Effecting his family. Panic sets in. He can't get away. *RUFF-RUFF-RUFF!* More biting. Crying. Whimpering.

Something's dying.

He understands.

It's just as it was before, with life being a punishing loop of perennial pain.

His surrogate mother is in serious trouble, he knows to interpret the pitch of her cries. *Bumf!* acts, he doesn't think, thinking is something long discarded into the metaphorical quicksand of humanhood.

He can't afford to.

Reflex is his animator.

His knuckles break the cheek of the waif girl, loosening the teeth under her supple flesh, forcing a line of blood to jetty from her slim mouth. Jumping up and out in a single bound, he moves, bestial in his litheness.

Although he's seen all matter of things in the cold, unforgiving world, he's never seen the likes of what writhes before him. Hissing, attacking.

The cats number in the dozens, ameliorating the dogs by the collective force of their quantity. They ripple, a suffocating blanket of claws and fangs, moving with a single mind, one large and determined cat brain.

Orange, black, white. Long-haired, short-haired, big-eared and folded-eared. From tabby to calico, from Burmese to Siamese to Bengal, they are all represented.

And they fight—*hard.*

Bumf! hears his dog mother suffering still, under six felines with sinking claws. He sees her fur open up, letting her spongy red meet fetid air.

Reacting to a mix of adrenaline and memory, the boy looks down. To his dismay...

There is no bottle this time.

With his heart tearing, he leaps for her, arms out, both grasping and seemingly violent. *Nnnnn... Nnnnn... Nnnnn.* His mother yowls as he peels them off, throwing the cats angrily against a brick wall.

Like parasites, they come away, and more and more of his rat terrier mother is unveiled.

If cancer pioneered the destruction of her mortal coil, then the myriad ribbons torn from her body, the fang punctures to her eyes, and the pieces of her jowls bitten off all served to expedite what it had started.

Death.

As plain as the mongrel rottweiler-dalmatian snapping a cat in two behind *Bumf!*

He pays no mind to the rallying of the pack, however, and instead kneels before his dog mother. Cradling her leaking head, the boy cries. Normal at first, displaying the mores of his human DNA, then doglike, howling between his mad sobs.

The fight is only just beginning between the litter and the pack. The boy is reminded of this when a claw slices through his cheek.

A Maine Coon.

It jumps and he snatches it in midair, opening his mouth wide to chomp. And that he does, crunching into the bones of the animal's face, which make a sound like a paper bag stomped beneath a boot.

The husk is pitched away as the boy turns, glimpsing his dogs biting cats, tearing them to veritable shreds, letting pieces and limbs fall away as they whip their heads.

A foreleg flings here. A hindquarter flings there.

The severed head of a bobtail rolls to the boy's feet.

The rat terrier mother might be gone, but her living children fight on. Lacerated all over their bodies, they will not let up. They're small, but they're as tough as woodpecker lips, just as they'd been taught.

Just as the world has shown them.

The pack's Doberman is foaming at the mouth, it bubbles forth red and white, spit sullied with blood.

It snaps, biting through the spine of a Persian.

The boy joins the fray now, fighting and biting and barking and growling.

Kicking his legs and swatting and loping from cat to cat, breaking their bodies, pulling their spirits out with his might. As their numbers dwindle, as cat carcasses and entrails repaint the dumping area behind the gas station, *she* emerges once more.

Bumf! hadn't noticed it prior to this, but the girl's short hair sticks up on both sides of her head, like cat ears. Her face is mottled too. With grime, but it almost looks like she has spots.

She hurdles, as graceful as a feline ballerina, falling before the boy. Panting, with chests bounding in and out, the two study one another.

Two inhabitants of opposing poles faced with opposing truths.

That of cats and of dogs and of everything in between, of *trying* to be human when everyone is just an animal deep down, or often, on the surface. The boy knows it. He knows how his parents beat and battered him.

He knows the bestial nature of mankind.

And he's found his own.

The only one that has made sense.

The only way that has provided love.

The way of the dog.

He is a dog.

And she… is a *cat*.

And he knows staring at her, loving her in those moments, seeing her femininity, her quiet yet dangerous grace, that they can never coexist. Just like his parents couldn't coexist. Cats and dogs don't belong together.

It's as plain as the guts being pulled from the poodle a few feet away.

They charge. Both parties hellbent on ending it. And they meet, smacking into one another with a world-echoing *pop*.

Yin and Yang tussle, rolling around among the dead dogs and cats, flipping over and kneeing and scratching and biting, until the boy gets the upper hand.

He rolls on top of the cat girl and he wraps his hands around her throat. He is not biting, he is not barking, he is not howling.

He is being a human as he kills her.

He is being a dog.

RJ Benetti is a horror author, living near a specific Great Lake in Pennsylvania. Growing up, he was always drawn to the spooky and the strange, and credits The Twilight Zone, Tales From the Crypt, The Simpsons' Treehouse of Horror episodes, Creepshow, Mars Attacks, Halloween, and The Shining for spurring his imagination and his love of storytelling.

He was recently nominated for the 2023 Splatterpunk Awards for his short story, Just Another Bloodbath at Camp Woe-Be-Gone (available on Amazon). He is also the 2022 Gross Out Contest Scares That Care champion. When he's not writing, he enjoys spending time doodling and watching horror movies with his girlfriend and long-haired chihuahua, named Dwight.

SHUCKING THE FLESH

MARK MJ GREEN

With the passing of the rain, the cobblestones sparkled and shone under the hazy glow of the gas lamps. One could almost believe London was a place of beauty, even here in Whitechapel, where the poor eked out a meagre existence and most laws were ignored or broken with little care toward their illegality.

One thing the recent downpour couldn't wash away was the stench that clung to the area like rot on a corpse. The cloying tang of faeces and urine created an unpleasant itch in Thomas' nose and he rubbed a gloved finger under it as if that would somehow deaden the cloying reek. His other hand rested on a simple-looking cane, although he appeared not to need the support, the item more accessory than necessity. He was huddled in a covered passageway, leaning beside the remnants of a peeling poster advertising a performing troupe at the Royal Aquarium in Westminster. On the floor beside him, amongst the blades of grass that had pushed through the dirt, and nestled amongst broken pieces of wood and torn scraps of cloth and paper, a sleeping, homeless man twitched and mumbled. A near-silent belch escaped the dreaming figure, the booze-soaked breath first filling his mouth then expanding his cheeks before slipping free in a flap of scab-encrusted lips.

One end of the passageway opens upon houses and a few other buildings, all tightly packed together, leaning into the street as if they quietly conspired with one another, whispering of the secret things that happen within, the weight of it all leaving them with a worn out look of near collapse. At the other end lay the main thoroughfare, which, if one chose to follow it, would lead through the City of London, over the Thames, and onward through Southwark and into Lambeth. Across the other side of the thoroughfare, opposite the passageway, squatted an unkempt courtyard; a lone tree surrounded by patchy overgrown grass and nettles grew at an awkward angle and the plump, ghostly forms of sleeping pigeons could be made out within the branches.

A few figures were visible at the edge of the light, lurking in the shadowy places, including one Thomas couldn't see but knew was present - his colleague Albert Frye. To call Albert large would be an understatement. It never ceased to amaze Thomas how his friend could veil his hulking form within the murky depths of shadow and silence.

Although Thomas and his snoring, homeless companion were both huddled in an area sheltered from the recent rainfall, the covered space was, somehow, still a home for dampness and things that dwelt in moisture. The brickwork appeared so sodden that it seemed to Thomas that if he were to use a finger to pick at the masonry, it would crumble beneath his touch. On the wall above the prone drunkard a snail made its slow journey, a faint slimy scrawl trailing behind it as it ventured perilously close to the sleeping man's face.

The street which had mostly emptied during the rainfall was

now beginning to fill with the usual nightly remnants of working folks and ne'er-do wells. Why so many of London's more undesirable elements operated at night always baffled Thomas. Understandably, the gloom could mask nefarious happenings, but operating on a diurnal pattern would create its own camouflage by appearing to be an act of the everyday law-abiding citizen. Or at least as law-abiding as anyone could be in these trying times. Not to mention how most people during the daytime were so wrapped up in their own world of poverty - particularly here in Whitechapel - that they cared not for the deeds of others. At night when folk scurried about, nervous, watching the shadows and those that moved within them, things were more readily observed due to the suspicious way they were undertaken that drew the eye, rather than avoided it. One of the denizens of the streets that Thomas recognised, not by experience, but certainly by reputation, was the figure of Molly Acton as she kept her short, plump form on the lookout for any gentleman willing to part with his coin for a taste of flesh.

A thin blanket of fog hovered above the ground, dampening ankles and trouser cuffs, swirling aside like a cautious ghost whenever someone passed through its ephemeral wrapping, or dancing in widdershins spirals as it was gathered up and spun around by the wheels of carriages and wagons.

A MUCOIDAL SNORT, thick and burbling, emanated from the sleeping man, causing Thomas to shift his gaze to look down at the decrepit figure. Drool had seeped from between the man's open lips, coating the unkempt growth of hair on his chin. Nearby, the snail continued its exploration, although it had turned away from the man and was now proceeding towards the roof of the archway, possibly driven away by the stink of alcohol and vomit-soused breath.

Thomas resumed his observation of the opposite courtyard just as a rectangle of light appeared when the door to a pub called The Warming Pan opened. The silhouetted form of a man, clearly well into his cups, stumbled into the filth of the unroofed rectangle of land. The rapid lurch the figure took from the door, coupled with a slight flail of the arms, spoke more of being pushed than leaving of his own volition. No sooner had he been ejected than the door slammed behind him, the fog muffling the sound. Inside the pub, the dim light visible through grease-smeared windows was snuffed out smothering the building in gloom. Staggering, the figure collided with one of the numerous piles of crates piled against the pub, and a cat, perched atop them grooming itself, let out a hiss of annoyance before leaping down and squeezing into a space between the wooden stacks.

A cart rattled along the road in a din of hooves upon cobbles, briefly obscuring Thomas' view. Once it had passed in a spray of water, filth and disturbed mist, Thomas could again see the drunken figure as it waved a bottle in the vague direction of the pub.

"I've no time to wait inside, I've no. . . no. . . God save the Queen." The drunkard's broken voice echoed around the brick courtyard as he sang a confused mish-mash of tunes. On hesitant feet that seemed to gain confidence as he moved, the drunk made his way to the road, changing songs again as he walked.

"Pop goes the weasel."

Smoothing down her clothing and pushing out her undeniably impressive bust, Molly made her move.

"Well, 'ello there, 'andsome. Looks like you could do with an 'and if you know what I mean?"

She took the drunk's arm in hers, pulling him against her chest.

Thomas failed to hear what other words passed between them as another cart rattled by. An agreement had undoubtedly been reached, as once the carriage had gone, the drunkard was fumbling at his trousers, trying to free himself, one hand, still grasping the bottle, struggling with the knot of rope that served as a belt, whilst the other groped at one of Molly's breasts. Either the man was too inebriated to realise or was too distracted by the allure of warm, soft flesh to care, as most locals knew Molly's reputation as a thief as well as a harlot.

"Come 'ere, let me 'elp you with that," she said, loosening his trousers and expertly emptying his pockets of valuables at the same time. With his coins and other sundries in her possession and the man with his trousers around his ankles and his cock dangling at half-mast, Molly shoved him onto his arse, hitched up her skirts to stop them from wrapping about her feet and ran off, laughing.

* * *

THERE WAS a whisper of movement overhead, no more than the ripple of silk on a gentle breeze, but enough to catch Thomas' attention as he had been listening out for it and knew that Jack had now arrived and was lurking on the shadowy rooftops. Jack's real name was unknown, but she had claimed her moniker after the character of Spring-Heeled Jack, who was the subject of various Penny Dreadfuls. Having travelled from Africa as a child, Jack never divulged the nature of her journey or what occurred to bring her to England's shores and to London. All Thomas knew was she was a damn fine agent.

The whistle of a wren sounded from above, Jack's signal that the target was almost here. From his hiding place within the courtyard, Albert responded in kind - message received and understood.

THOMAS relaxed and let the sounds of London wash over him: The rattle of the approaching wagon. The phlegmy, sickly breathing of the homeless man. Angered shouts of two men in argument in a nearby street. The distant cry of a woman screaming before the sound abruptly cuts short and somewhere, far away, the shrill wail of a policeman's whistle could be heard, others soon answering in piercing notes.

The fog had thickened, shifting from a wispy coverlet to a thick apparitional miasma that swirled like a living thing as the carriage emerged like a spirit from one of Dickens' tales. A single lantern burned above the driver, the dim luminance casting a glow upon the surrounding fog. Despite the decreased visibility, Thomas could discern the white ribbon tied to the doors of the carriage, declaring its ownership to the gang known as the Whitechapel Wilders. Despite being one of the newer gangs, they had swiftly eradicated any opposition in the district and supposedly had dealings with criminals in other parts of the city. What made them stand out, at least as far as Thomas and the other agents were concerned, was the rumour of their involvement in things of a mystical nature. Whether their supernatural dealings were fabricated as a way of creating an air of danger about them or held the truth of devilish dabblings remained to be seen and was why they were kept under watch this night. Although the Wilder's dealings with mysticism bore the appearance of boisterous gangland swagger, a few whispered details had circulated that carried the faintest slivers of truth.

The driver climbed down, as did another figure who had been hanging unseen to the side of the carriage. This second man had a cloth wrapped around one hand and even through the murk, a red-brown stain of dried blood was visible, soaked into the impromptu bandage. The pair held a muttered conversation, their words swirling like the tendrils of fog, making their speech sound broken so that only the occasional word bore any clarity. Not even Jack, hidden on the rooftops above the men, could make out all they discussed; their discourse obscured by the snorting breath of the horse and the sounds emanating from within the cart: muffled whines, punctuated by the occasional staccato bark and the mournful howls of animals lost and in fear.

From his position under the archway, Thomas could not see inside the carriage when the two men opened it. Nor could Albert from where he sheltered unseen and unnoticed but, from above, Jack was able to observe the interior, filled with crates, though sight wasn't needed to detect the volumetric increase of the whines and barks.

Grabbing a crate, the driver entered the courtyard, moving toward a nondescript house only a few doors from The Warming Pan. With his hands burdened, he kicked at the door: a few sharp, irate blows to signal someone to open it for him. His companion, with the bandaged hand, also picked up a cage from the carriage and followed the driver.

Molly's inebriated dalliance had dragged himself from the floor and was trying to pull his breeches back on. Somehow, he had managed to put both feet into a single trouser leg and swayed even more precariously than before.

The house door opened, dim candlelight revealing a child who stood aside as the driver stomped inside. Two other children emerged from the house, making their way through the courtyard toward the wagon.

Bandage-Hand was halfway to the house when the drunkard became further entangled in his clothing and, unable to stay vertical, fell into his path. The pair collided, and the crate, no more than a wooden base with a crude wireframe, crashed to the floor.

"Watch where you're going, you bleedin' wanker," Bandage-Hand spat crudely.

Looking down, the thug realised the dropped cage had split apart, wire separating from wood. A small dog was trying urgently to squeeze through the gap. It had managed to get its head out the opening and was wiggling its shoulders through when Bandage-Hand noticed.

"Where you think you're goin', you ratbag?"

With one heavily booted foot, he kicked at the cage and sent it tumbling end over end, animal and all.

The struggling dog cried in pain, the sound not too dissimilar from that of a squalling babe.

Ignoring the drunk, who had managed to pull up his trousers and was making a hasty retreat, the gangster walked over to the mangled wreckage of dog and cage. The wire was dented and buckled and the impact had sent the animal tumbling free from its prison. Unlike the drunk, it hadn't managed to limp to safety, being only able to pull itself along by its front legs, the back ones dragging uselessly behind it; the impact having broken the poor creature's spine. It whined pitifully as it hauled itself along, the fog giving it an ethereal, nightmarish appearance. The man lumbered over to the maimed animal. It wasn't the same dog that had bitten his hand earlier that night, but his ire was up and he felt the need to take it out on something. Looming over the terrified animal he raised a boot above its head, intending to stamp its skull into bloody fragments.

Above Bandage-Hand, a sound no louder than the whisper of moth wings ruffled the mist as Jack silently dropped behind him. She pulled him toward her, dragging him off balance and preventing him from crushing the head of the wounded dog. The blade of a thin stiletto knife punctured his carotid artery and he fell to the ground trailing a crimson arc in his wake. The light from the gas lamps, reflecting eerily from the fog, gave the arterial spray an unusual pinkish haze.

From within the vaporous cloud of fog, the two urchins who had appeared from inside the house froze in their tracks, mouths agape at the sight of Bandage-Hand's body bleeding out the last of its life onto the cobbles.

Jack was crouched beside the injured pup, softly stroking its flank and speaking in a hushed, soothing voice. From behind the children, the figure of the driver emerged. He was in the process of yelling at them for slacking off when he spotted Jack and his now-deceased colleague. Loosening a heavy-looking cudgel from his belt he raised it over his right shoulder, widening his stance for balance.

There was a thudding of heavy footsteps, the sound warped by the fog and the enclosed nature of the courtyard created the illusion of it coming from all directions at once.

A huge form tore through the swirling mist and emitting a thunderous bellow, the brutish figure of Albert Frye burst into view like a demon emerging from the smoke of Hell's chimneys. He crashed into the driver, scooping him from his feet and carrying the surprised figure before him. The driver's cudgel clattered noisily to the ground, followed by a crushing impact as Albert rammed the man into a brick wall, the driver's rib bones crunching and splintering from the impact.

Releasing the now unconscious figure, Albert let it tumble like a broken marionette whilst Jack removed her coat, gently wrapping it around the injured dog; continuing her whispered litany of soothing words. Despite its trauma, the animal flicked out a small pink tongue, licking at Jack's fingers, tickling her skin and causing an oft-hidden smile to tug at her lips. Having left the shelter of the covered alleyway, Thomas hunkered beside Jack and the two children, whilst Albert, not wanting his size to intimidate the youngsters, kept a respectable distance. They had probably witnessed enough horror in their short lives and having seen him bellow like a possessed beast and crush a man, made Albert wary of scaring them further.

"Are you children okay?" Thomas asked. One of them, a boy, nodded whilst the other, a young, grubby-faced girl, spoke.

"We're alright, 'ent we?" she said to her companion, the words more of a statement of affirmation, rather than a question. "Who are you, sir?"

"We're here to help," Thomas replied. "We want to stop the Wilders from hurting any more of the animals. And the children," he added. "Can you tell us what we will find inside? How many people?"

"Only one other kid like us, sir," the girl replied. "One more Wilder in the butchery with him, sir."

"Butchery?" Jack asked.

"Aye. It's where they bring the dogs, miss. We skins 'em and Wilders takes the fur and what's left into the basement. It's where the other folks are. The Robes, we calls 'em."

"The Robes? Who are they?"

"Don't rightly know, miss; they all go downstairs and speaks odd." The girl gestured toward her silent companion. "George here said they's doing evil. He saw once, and they cut out his tongue. It's why he don't say much, miss."

George, having been introduced, smiled and opened his mouth, revealing the mangled and cauterised stump that remained of his tongue.

Albert broke his silence. "I've heard enough. These Robes sound like the ones we're after. Even if they're not, anyone who kicks dogs and maims children needs to be dealt with."

"Agreed," Thomas replied, finger tapping upon his cane while he thought. He turned back to the girl.

"How many of these Robes are there?"

Her eyebrows narrowed as she concentrated then she held up her hands, all fingers extended and spread.

"This many."

AFTER DISCUSSING THE MATTER, the group agreed that Jack would return the cart, along with the children and the dogs still caged within, to headquarters. Much to her chagrin, the children seemed to have latched onto her. Whether it was her soft treatment toward the injured pup that drew them toward her was hard to say. The pair seemed comfortable in her presence, especially George who had tried to hold her hand at one point, much to Jack's surprise.

Whilst Jack headed out, Thomas and Albert would enter the building and investigate further. They would try not to engage until Jack returned, hopefully with backup.

Picking up the injured dog as gently as possible, Jack climbed onto the driver's seat with the children, placing the wounded animal in George's lap. With a flick of the reins and a click of her tongue, they disappeared into the drifting fog.

Checking his cane and revolver, Thomas, and Albert who needed no weapon other than his fists, entered unopposed through the still-open door. The stench of blood, spilt bowels and death assaulted them. Hooked chains, mercifully bare excepting a few streaks of blood or the occasional strands of fur, hung throughout the room affixed to the wooden rafters. The dirt-covered floor had become clumped together in places, accumulations of blood and shit having collected amongst it, dried into hard lumps of putrefaction. There were brush streaks among the dirt, signs that someone, no doubt one of the children, had attempted to clean the filth but had been mostly unsuccessful.

A figure moved at the other side of the room where there stood a table covered in dried blood. Knives used for skinning and butchery were strewn upon its scratched and filthy surface. Next to the table, another member of the Wilders had grabbed a dog and casually, mercilessly stabbed it onto one of the hooks. The sharp metal had punctured the dog through the scruff, leaving the animal squealing with inconceivable agony. Its scream, pitiful and agonising, wrenched through the building, confusion and pain entwining as one echoed from the walls.

Beside the man, a young boy stood frozen, a knife in one hand.

"Do your job and gut the beast, boy." The Wilder grabbed the child, his hand crushing the back of the youngster's neck, squeezing it as he directed him toward the crying dog. A bucket, stained dark from countless outpouring of animal life squatted below the crying animal. The boy was weeping, now too, tears leaving clear tracks down the filth on his face; etches of pain upon the dirt of suffering. The gutting knife wobbled in his shaking hand, the point dancing around as he neared the suspended dog.

"Do it," the Wilder threatened. "Do it or I'll take yer eye like I took that other brat's tongue."

The child, terrified of what refusal would bring him, pressed the point of the blade against the short fur below the dog's soft, pink belly. The cries from the animal increased and the distraught child tried to step away. The thug grabbed him once more, this time also gripping a hand over that of the child's, clamping it in place and forcing him to push the knife-point through the skin of the dog, slicing it up to its chin, entrails spilling out in a rush of foulness and heat as they tumbled into the awaiting bucket.

The animal bucked and twitched, trying to bite the hand that was hurting it, but its body, already weakened and being overcome by shock, slipped from consciousness, then from life.

The brutish Wilder then turned his attention to the boy, twisting him around to face him, holding the bloodied knife with the point toward the youngster's eye.

"I told yer I would take thine eye, boy, so now -"

His words ended. His eyes bulged, his mouth opening and closing. The knife he had been threatening the boy with slipped from slack fingers, thumping to the dirt floor. Behind the thug stood Thomas. He had loosened the hidden blade from his cane and with expert precision, thrust it into the back of the man's neck. With a swift flex of his wrist, Thomas severed the spinal cord, the man collapsing to the floor, conscious but unable to move.

"You are safe now, boy," Thomas said. "I would suggest you take leave of this place. However," he pointed toward the prone Wilder. "This man is still alive and will feel the pain of anything you inflict upon him, should you choose to do so."

Albert approached in a clatter of chains as his bulk brushed against the hanging loops of metal.

"Sorry we couldn't save the pup, lad," he jabbed a thumb toward the collapsed Wilder. "We feared he would have heard us if we moved any quicker, and then we may have lost you n'all."

The boy sniffed and wiped the back of his hand under his nose, the mucus making another clear trail through the dirt that stained his face.

"Do you know of the ones known as The Robes?" Thomas asked.

The boy nodded.

"Where can we find them?"

Turning, the boy pointed toward a corner of the room where an iron handle fitted to a wooden floor hatch was visible.

"Downstairs," he mumbled.

"Thank you," said Thomas. "Now, be about your business but do not tarry here, for it is not safe."

The boy nodded again, watching as the two men approached the hatch. Once they had carefully opened it and descended out of sight, he picked up the knife and stared at the helpless Wilder lying on the floor.

***

THE STEPS LEADING under the house were nothing more than roughly hewn slabs hacked from the dirt and layered with planks of wood across the top and front for support. They descended for around eight feet before levelling out into a corridor that matched their appearance of crude construction. Alcoves had been inexpertly scooped out along the wall and lanterns set within them, casting enough luminance for the men to see by. Further along, at what was presumably the corridor's end, the flickering glow of flames was visible through the jaggedly hewn opening, the light sending strange shadows dancing and convulsing around the entranceway. Accompanying the chimerical flickering, voices could be heard chanting in unison. Strange and indecipherable, the words felt wrong, twisting senses so that it felt as if the listener's ears were impossibly trying to decipher hieroglyphic imagery.

At first, when descending into the stygian murk, the stench of death from the upper butchery had cleared, replaced by the petrichor of damp earth, but as Thomas and Albert drew closer to the shifting, dreamlike shadows, the blemish of rotten meat became almost overpowering.

The nearer they approached the louder chanting became, whether by proximity or the fervour of the susurrating choristers was impossible to tell. The unpleasant speech contained no words the pair recognised if indeed they were words and not a syncopated coagulation of the known, warped into a sense of the infernal and diabolic.

Closer the pair approached and thus the sickly fetor of corruption and decay increased in unpleasantness; a perfume of putrefaction so thick upon the air it had a cloying, oily texture, causing the two men to cover their faces, attempting to spare their insides from its essence.

Despite the strange wretchedness of it all and the unshakeable sense of despairing misery, and pain, they were ill-prepared for the sight that befell them as they reached the corridor's end and found themselves in the chamber beyond.

ALMOST A DOZEN FIGURES stood around the large room, each draped in a cloak of dark blue. Beneath their capes, the bodies of the gathered men and women were unclothed, lost in their own personal ecstasies. The men's members stood proud, many with stringy fluid depending grossly from them like gossamer slime as they caressed themselves, hands rubbing at engorged flesh. The women, too, were enwrapped in demented arousal, their thighs glistening in the flickering light with not just sweat but also from carnal secretions as fingers pleasured cunts.

It was in the centre of the room though, where the true nightmare lay. Dozens, no hundreds, of dogs, flayed and profaned, their remains stacked in a blasphemous hillock of unimaginable anguish and desecration.

The chanting reached an explosive finale, as did the self-pleasure of the gyrating figures. Their nightmarish utterances ended, replaced by groans of orgiastic pleasure, many of the men close enough to the corpse pile that their ejaculated seed spattered upon the flayed carcasses; one more humiliation upon the dead canines.

As groans of gratification quietened, a single booming report filled the underground lair as a round from Thomas' gun smashed into the nearest man's skull, exiting his face in a shower of bone fragments and gore.

Stunned by the deafening interruption and still in the throes of climax, it took a moment for the cloaked figures to react. The woman nearest to the deceased man had at first thought it was a warm spurt of passion that had spattered upon her, it was only when her neighbour collapsed and what remained of his thoughts and dreams slopped from his head that her eyes fell upon Thomas and Albert.

The two men had expected the death to create terror and confusion. Being met by anger was not something either had been prepared for.

"Fools. What have you done?"

The Beaumont-Adams revolver fired again, the .442 calibre round punching a hole just above the woman's eye, felling her instantly.

Another figure, cock shrivelling like a frightened creature seeking escape, raised his hands in what he must have thought was a placatory gesture.

"Stop! The ritual is incomplete. The great Shuck is not -"

There was another booming report, though this issued from no spark igniting gunpowder, but rather from within the room itself, a bestial growl of death twisted into the pained cry of birth.

Sprouting from the pile of flayed corpses, an immense dog head appeared, its teeth clamping onto the man, who barely managed to scream before the jaws snapped shut, crushing flesh and bone; bursting him apart in an explosion of carnage.

As the gathered people stared in horror, Thomas realised the true nature of the abomination birthed from the mound of carcasses. The hellish beast hadn't appeared from within them; it was them. Its body was an abomination crafted from the assemblage of flayed animals and the mounds of rotten offal. The fangs protruding from its gums were jagged splinters of bone, the jaws the fused carcasses of deceased animals. A flayed paw dangled from its chin, the beast an abomination of discarded scraps creating something from the memory of a shape they once shared. More of the bodies began to integrate themselves into creating the monstrous being. Bones and skin stitching and fusing as they became an amalgamation of the whole, entrails being dragged into the body, bulking it out with the reeking, flashy garbage. Two skulls, trailing scraps of mouldering meat, slid up the hound's face until they entered the hollow spaces of the eye sockets where they burst into flame.

The cultists either stood, gaping in awe and terror, or had

dropped to their knees, prostrating themselves before the crea-ture, the dark God they had sought to bend to their control. A few, having less courage, or perhaps a better sense of self-preser-vation than their fellows, chose to either run or hide.

Albert grabbed Thomas' sleeve.

"I think we should leave," he said.

"Agreed," Thomas replied.

The pair dashed back down the corridor as fast as they could, reaching the steps and hurrying to the main floor of the building. Behind them, a cultist tried to take flight the same way only to be consumed by a gout of fire that ignited his robe, the material melting to his skin as his flesh scorched to charcoal.

A sound that was a combination of bestial roar and demonic howl bellowed from the chamber, the ululating sound pursuing Thomas and Albert as they ran.

Crashing through the floor hatch the pair scrambled into the main building, both spotted the body of the once paralysed Wilder lying on the floor where they had left him. The only difference was that he no longer lived, the knife jammed to the handle now jutting from an eye socket, the remaining urchin no longer present.

HURTLING OUTSIDE, trying to maintain their balance on the damp cobblestones, the pair headed for the street, where, through the thinning fog, they could see the glow of lanterns hanging from a waiting carriage.

Jack was sitting in the driver's seat and as the two men sprinted her way she was about to question them, but her inquiry faltered as the house burst apart in an explosion of wood, brick and cast iron, showering the area in broken timber and masonry and the shredded remains of the cultists who had foolishly sought to commune with powers they did not understand, nor could ever control.

The stray cat had returned to its favoured hunting ground but didn't have time to regret its choice as a giant paw, constructed from the remains of flayed dogs, crashed down, crushing the animal and the stack of crates it sat upon into a splintered mess. The bowed tree (now empty of roosting avians who had taken clumsy flight at the first sounds of the beast), fell to the floor.

"I see you boys have been stirring up trouble as usual," Jack shouted as the breathless figures reached the carriage and hurriedly clambered aboard.

"We do seem to have a knack for it," rumbled Albert.

"It seems you may have outdone yourselves this time."

"I'm inclined to agree," answered Thomas. He gestured down the street with his cane. "Shall we?"

Jack flicked the reins and the two horses - on the verge of panic as the odour of death and the sounds of destruction filled the air - galloped away.

ENRAGED by the sight of the fleeing figures, nostrils filled with the scent of fear and flesh emanating from the terrified horses, and knowing only pain, the hound shook itself free of the building's remains and gave chase.

"I DON'T SUPPOSE you brought backup?" Thomas shouted, the rush of air whipping his words away from his lips.

"In the back," Jack replied as behind them, another structure split apart as the hell-beast crashed into the street. The crimson glow from its dog-skull eyes reflecting from the rain-slick stonework and the swirling mist creating an infernal ambience.

In the rear of the carriage was a repeating rifle imported from America, a coach gun, and an assortment of ammunition.

"Somehow, I think this won't be enough," muttered Albert.

"I was expecting a handful of cultists, not whatever that is," replied Jack, having heard Albert's words even over the noise of their flight. "Next time, I'll pack a howitzer."

A howl rent the air and the crimson glow from the hound's burning eyes set the fog ablaze as the monster surged closer; the carmine glimmer shining upon the carriage and its occupants gave them a blood-smeared appearance. With a crack, Thomas began firing the rifle, the lever action making reloading swift. Shot after shot struck the hound as all seven rounds struck home with seemingly no effect,

"Thomas! Take over!" yelled Jack.

Sliding into the driver's seat, Thomas took the reins, the horses still requiring no encouragement to run from the creature pursuing them.

A boom reverberated as Albert fired the coach gun, both barrels ejecting a spray of pellets at the beast.

As they continued their headlong dash, the citizens on the streets screamed and sought refuge, fleeing from the maddened horses and the pursuing demon. The noise of the chase and the gunfire reverberating from the walls of buildings lining the streets, a mobile wall of roiling noise warning all to keep away.

Jumping into the back of the wagon whilst Albert reloaded, Jack ran across the floor of the rocking conveyance and leapt out the rear directly at the dog. She somersaulted in the air, landing upon the carcasses that comprised the animal's neck and drew a pepperbox pistol from her coat; one hand gripping the dead fur of its nape, the other pressing the rotating barrel point blank against the hound. Jack squeezed the trigger. There was a blast of gunpowder and a cloud of smoke and Jack pulled back the hammer once more, firing round after round until the weapon ran dry.

The animal yowled, the sound more like that of an angry bear than the whimper of a wounded dog as it slid to a halt, claws scraping upon the wet cobbles.

Not waiting for the creature to retaliate, Jack bunched her legs under her and leapt upward to a nearby building, just managing to grasp an outcropping of stone and haul herself to the roof.

Struggling against the terrified horses, Thomas pulled at the reins, slowing the fear-maddened animals enough for he and Albert to jump from the carriage which continued clattering away once they were clear. Looking around, Thomas spotted a butcher shop and gestured toward the half-carcass of a pig dangling in the window. "Grab that," he shouted to Albert. "I have an idea."

Not wasting time with questions, Albert ran to the shop window and smashed the glass with a single blow from the butt of his shotgun.

***

IN THE BLOODY glow of the fog, Thomas could see the hound rearing up, its gigantic head searching for Jack, nostrils seeking her scent. Hoping he wasn't about to get himself killed, Thomas shouted at the beast.

"Bad dog!"

The hound ceased its searching and shifted focus to the figure approaching it.

"Bad dog!" Thomas repeated. "Down!"

Though created by ungodly ritual, the beast was still, in essence, a dog and finding itself unable to disobey, it lowered itself to the ground, ears flattening against its skull.

From the rooftop, Jack looked down in bewildered astonishment, trying to decide if Thomas was brave, lucky, reckless, or a combination of all three.

"You do not run off down the street," Thomas continued in his admonishment, pointing a finger at the giant hound. "That is bad."

To his relief and astonishment, the dog hunkered down onto the street and then rolled onto its side. Now beside the creature, Thomas gently ran his hand under the dog's chin, trying to ignore how it was a melding of deceased canines.

"You have to be a good boy," he said, his voice taking on a more soothing tone. "Yes, you do. You have to be a good boy."

Behind the dog, a tail crafted from a horrific melding of legs and sinew thumped on the ground.

"That's right. Good boy."

The appendage thumped again, repeating the motion.

Slowly, having lowered herself to the ground, Jack approached.

"Tell me it isn't wagging its tail," she said rhetorically.

"He is because he's a good boy. You are a good boy, aren't you?" Thomas replied, still making a fuss of the giant animal.

The dog's nostrils twitched and it sat up.

Albert approached carrying not one but two pig halves slung over his shoulders.

"This has got to be the craziest thing I have ever seen," he said.

The dog licked its lips, although, like the rest of its construction, the tongue was a mish-mash of combined parts and for a moment it had looked as if it was spewing out a tangle of thick, intestinal rope until the trio realised what it was.

"Wait," Thomas commanded the dog, holding up a hand, palm outward.

Albert dropped the pork to the floor and stepped away.

"Wait," Thomas said once more as blood-smeared drool escaped the dog's mouth.

"Good boy. Come on then, eat up," Thomas called enthusiastically as he gestured toward the hunks of meat. After looking at him momentarily, the dog stood up, tail still wagging as it approached the porcine slabs and picked one up, chewing it whole. As it did so, the forms that comprised it sloughed away, becoming almost liquid as they collapsed upon themselves.

After a few minutes, the amalgam of flayed animals was gone, only a single, normal-sized dog remaining where a monster once stood. It looked up at the trio. In its eyes, a glimmer of crimson sparkled.

Crouching down, Albert held out his hand, palm upward and inviting. The dog wandered over, sniffed the proffered fingers and began licking them, causing a rumbling laugh to roll from the large man.

"Good boy," he said.

The dog rolled onto its back, exposing its underside, and Albert began scratching at its belly and chest, causing one of the dog's legs to kick.

The big man laughed again.

"So, what now?" asked Jack.

Smiling, Thomas looked at the scene before them. "Now? Now we retrieve the cart, put that meat in the back, return to headquarters, fill out reports and get some rest.

"What about the dog?" Jack queried. "Will it change back again?"

"No idea," replied Albert. "Probably. But I think that as long as he is well looked after, he will be fine. He's a good boy."

He scratched the dog behind the ear, smiling as its tail wagged with joy whilst the sounds and smells of London surrounded him with comforting familiarity.

One thing was true about life in the capital: it was certainly never dull.

Bald, bearded and bumbling, Mark likes the spooky side of life and things that go bump in the night. Although that's usually him wandering into something as he didn't bother to turn a light on.

Mark writes horror stories in a variety of styles within the genre and enjoys spending time with his family - including his day who may, or may not, be demonic.

He's also a bit of a nerd and when he hasn't got his face buried in a book can be found playing video games and board games.

Take one Mr Potatohead. Attach his angry eyes - preferably placing one of them at a slightly different angle to the other. Affix a beard and leave the head barren of growth.

Congratulations. You now have your very own **Mark M.J. Green.**

Caution: Product may swear at random moments and for no apparent reason.

HER FUR ON MY LIPS

JAE MAZER

The carpet tastes like ash in a Styrofoam cup. It's just stale, I know—a layer of dust, hair, and sloughed-off human flesh as fine and translucent as onion skin. These are all normal things, things that disperse via air from furnace through a house that has lived a lifetime. So many hairs, so much dust, so much skin.

And here I am, tongue lolling on a virtually untouched carpet as I pant, inhaling what I'd never ever vacuum off this carpet in a closet that never ever gets use. A year ago, my parents stayed in here, and since then, my dad died and my mother no longer wants to travel, not by herself. My siblings stay at hotels with my many nieces and nephews, and my friends all live around here in their own homes, with their own basement carpets that taste like dust and hair and flesh.

Beside me, Juno pants. It's silent, though, not like my gasping for air. Being a dog, she's had much more experience panting than I have.

"Good girl," I whisper, and she licks my face.

I wince in pain.

Her eyes widen, showing the whites.

"It's okay," I say as I pat her on the rump.

Juno's tail wags, but I rest my hand on it. I don't want it to thump the walls. I don't want them to know where we are.

Juno is a good dog. Big and silver and saturated with love and hope.

Juno licks my face again. She's telling me everything will be okay. I want to believe it, I do, but my body tells me otherwise. The taste of copper in my mouth, the swollen slit of my eye where very little light could get through if there were any light in the basement closet. Gooseflesh ripples over my skin, reminding me of my nakedness. Naked, wet, numb.

Juno curls in closer, pressing her body against mine, sharing her heat and taking deep breaths to coax me away from a panic attack. I slow my panting and match her rhythm, breathing in, out, in, out, until my heart is no longer a thundering staccato against my splintered ribs. I close my eyes and bury my face in her fur, allowing her scent to carry me away to a more blissful moment.

"JUST OPEN IT," he said.

I sat there on the couch with the wrapped box in my lap. I couldn't imagine what it might possibly be. We just spent a fortune on our wedding and honeymoon.

"What is this for?" I asked.

"You!" he said.

I wanted to be mad at him for wasting money and for giving me a gift for no occasion. We needed to save money. New house, new marriage, new careers. Everything was shiny-new and scary, and I didn't want to mess it up.

He looked at me with those wide eyes, that crooked smile, and that unruly coil of hair than hung down the side of his forehead, and I realized that anger at him was impossible.

"Open it," he said as he bounced on the balls of his feet, anticipation thick like Christmas Eve.

I undid the gold bow wrapped around the box—no easy feat with my too-long French manicure I had done for our wedding. With bow tossed aside, I lifted the lid and found more gold within.

"What ..."

My breath hitched in my throat. I plucked the gold fabric out of the box and held it up into the light. Even though it was really just yellow, it twinkled metallic through my swelling tears.

"What?!" I shrieked as tears spilled down my face, the salty fluid wetting my gaping smile.

I leapt from the couch with the dog collar in my hand as he bent down and picked the puppy up from her hiding spot behind the love seat. He held her out to me, the chub of her face smooshing her eyes closed as his massive hands cradled her as tenderly as his excitement would allow.

I grabbed her and cuddled her to my chest. I fell to my knees, crying and laughing, and she licked my face, cleaning away the tears.

"Really!" I squealed.

"Really," he said as he knelt beside me and put his arm around us. "Can't have a house without a dog!"

We sure couldn't. And it was no longer a house. With Juno there, it had become a home.

JUNO'S FUR is still as soft as the day we got her. Laying here in this closet, with my eyes closed and her body against me, I listen close to her breathing, imagining that first night when she slept on her brand-new dog bed, little puffs of snores coming out of her mouth as my husband and I made love by the fire.

Yes, there. I want to stay in that memory.

I try to imagine his body against mine, both of us warm and sweaty and overcome with pleasure. But reality will not let me forget. It isn't sweat I feel over my body but blood and vomit. It isn't seismic release I feel between my legs but the sting and ache of a gash torn from tailbone to belly button, my insides hanging outside, vaginal fluids pooling on this dusty fucking carpet along with my own shit and blood.

I had never been raped before tonight.

A door upstairs closes. I wish that Juno had not a paw but a hand to press over my mouth to keep my screams quiet. I've done a good job so far, but I can't last forever. The threat is outside the closet, and the bedroom, and all the way up the stairs, but there is a threat close by. Anxiety swells like an erection inside of me, threatening to split me in two and announce itself with an explosion and a scream. But I must stay silent, both for Juno and myself.

I wonder why it matters. Nobody is getting out of here alive.

A low whine hums in Juno's throat.

"It's okay, girl," I lie.

She licks blood off my face. I don't have the heart to show her I'm covered. We're both covered. Pressed up against her, I've transferred my gore to her silver fur, caking it a muddy brown. I can't imagine how it smells to her sensitive nose.

I hear shuffling from above. I hold my breath, listening. Voices. Men. The two men that broke into my home. I hear doors opening and closing. They are looking for me.

I can still feel their meat inside me, tearing me, hear their laughter like dissonant bells clanging inside my skull.

I gasp a sob, and dust puffs up in front of my face. Juno nestles in closer and presses her head on my throat as if to say, *Be quiet, Mom. It's okay, Mom.*

Her pressure gives me comfort. It always did.

WITH MY TODDLER finally tucked away in bed and my infant latched to my nipple, I sat on the couch and cried. I let it all out, bathing my weeks-old baby in tears while my nipples split beneath her suction. Exhaustion made me woozy, as if I'd downed the myriad Hurricanes of my youth. But I was no longer on Bourbon Street. I was in my house with the walls folding in like cards as routine and monotony and physical deprivation ground me into dust.

"I love my babies," I told Juno, who was curled up on the other end of the couch, watching me with her big brown eyes. "I do."

Juno came to me, like she always did, and carefully maneuvered around the baby to nuzzle into my throat. I rested my head on hers and soaked her with my tears.

"I thought motherhood would be beautiful," I cried. "I thought I would gain angels, not lose friends, and my body, and my sex life, and my career."

Juno listened, like she always did.

"I'm so tired," I continued, babbling now, with snot pouring from my nose and tears gushing from my eyes. "Always crying, always wanting. And it wouldn't bother me if I wasn't so tired. And hungry. I want to just sit on my fucking ass to eat. To shit without someone watching, to move through the house without someone always touching, speaking, tugging, wailing."

I didn't have meltdowns like this often, but when I did, everything came crashing down, suffocating me in a pile of diapers, dirty laundry, scattered toys.

Still, Juno listened.

"My friends are out drinking lemon drops, all dressed up in jeans and sparkly tops. I can't wear jeans because my belly spills over the band, and none of my tops fit anymore, and my husband won't even touch me, not that I want him to ..."

Juno licked my face. I looked down at her, and her tail wagged, whapping against the couch cushion in silly percussion. I pressed my forehead to hers, and she let me stay there as the clock ticked on, the baby suckled, and the chores waited.

"The house is so quiet in the middle of the night," I said. "But I don't get rest. I don't get a night like the rest of the world. Night is supposed to be the end of the day, a shutdown, a break until the routine starts again. It's never true night for a mother."

Juno slid her head off mine and rested in on my chest and on the baby. My daughter's face was peace and perfection. And I knew it was all worth it.

"I'm just tired," I repeated, then kissed Juno and my baby on their foreheads.

JUNO'S COMPANIONSHIP had kept me alive and sane through two pregnancies, two children, and now tonight. It doesn't matter what I was upset over, or how scared I was, how happy. It doesn't matter if I break things, or mess things up, or neglect to do a million little things. She adores me no matter what.

We are the perfect family. Him, the kids, me, Juno. Loving through the struggles, euphoric through the good time.

Were. *Were* a perfect family.

Another sob. This time, Juno puts her face over mine, muffling the noise with her fur. I wrap my arms around her and give her a hug. She shivers and whines, more air than noise but I still hear the pain. She has lost everything too. We both have. Everything but each other.

"Oohhhh, someone's gonna be a mommy!" I squealed.

I patted Juno's head and gave her a hug. My husband looked terrified.

"It's okay," I said. "It's just puppies."

"But," he stammered. "How ... is she just gonna ..."

He made a motion with his hands at his crotch, emulating what I could only imagine was birth.

"Yes," I said. "Girls push babies out of their vaginas. You remember?"

He rolled his eyes.

"I don't know how this happened," he said, shaking his head.

"I do," I said. "Dick goes in cunt, and—"

"EW!" he shrieked. "They're dogs!"

"Works the same, babe."

"I mean, how ... who did this to her?" he asked.

I shrugged. "Gimli's always sneaking under that fence."

"He's not fixed?" he asked.

"Evidently not."

The neighbour's dog was Juno's best friend. They liked running around together, swimming in the pool, and, it turned out, fucking when no one was looking.

"It'll be great," I said as I took Juno's face in my hands and kissed her forehead. "She'll be a good mom."

And she was. She had a healthy litter of six and tended to them every second of every day. When she was exhausted, dragging her feet with her eyes drooping closed, I would have her lay on her bed and cover her with her favorite yellow blanket while I took the puppies in the other room to play with them while she got rest. While they were nursing, ripping at Juno's nipples like feral hogs, I would lay next to her, stroke her fur, and kiss her forehead. Her tail would wag, and I would smile.

I REACH OVER and grab Juno's yellow blanket. Luckily, it was on the bed in the basement bedroom when Juno and I were running to hide. It's the cleanest thing in this closet; the scent from the lavender laundry beads is a welcome reprieve from the bodily fluids and fear that permeates the small space.

There is still movement upstairs. They are not leaving. I have been trying not to think about it, but now I must.

"They won't leave," I whisper to Juno. "Not with me alive. They can't leave a witness."

Another whine, and Juno's eyes turn to the faint light seeping through the crack at the opening of the closet.

"If we stay here, they'll find us. And we won't live to tell about it."

I think of life outside that basement closet. My body is broken, fucked and beaten to shreds. My mind is broken too. Juno isn't hurt. She doesn't know the horror that lays splayed out on the floor above. My heart aches at the thought of her seeing the carnage.

What am I going to do?

How will I get out of the house with Juno?

But those aren't the thoughts nagging for attention. The ones screaming at me, coaxing out the panic.

What will I do after? Once I'm safe, and healed, and life begins again?

Life. What's left?

I force a memory. I have to see it, to taste it, to feel it in order to truly, deeply understand what is waiting for me in the coming days, weeks, months, years.

Nothing.

IT ALL HAPPENED SO FAST. Little did I know that in an hour, I would be cowering in a basement closet, having lost my entire world.

I was cooking dinner at the stove. Homemade mac and cheese, my son's favourite. My daughter didn't prefer it, but I added bacon to hers so she'd gobble it down. That girl loves bacon.

My son was watching YouTube at the table on his tablet. He was laughing at some guy who was teaching his dog to go down a slide. He wanted to show me the video, so I looked, and I was laughing too. Genuine joy at the sound of my son's laughter. In the living room, my husband danced with my daughter in his arms. She'd just started kindergarten, and the other kiddos at school had taught her how to twerk. She was attempting to teach my husband. He looked like he was having a seizure. I laughed at this too, and at the peals of laughter blasting from my daughter.

It was a symphony of pure joy. The pasta bubbling on the stove, my son's video, the thumping of my husband's feet as he attempted to dance, my daughter's laughter.

The backdoor smashed open as if it was a conductor's baton silencing the entire orchestra.

My husband and I looked at each other. Our smiles faded.

Suddenly, there were men in my house. They both seemed larger than possible—giant yetis stalking us with talons and teeth—but in reality, they were no bigger than my husband. I didn't panic. Not yet. It wasn't real, it was unbelievable, a dark magical illusion.

My daughter screamed at the sight of them, and my husband scooped her up in his arms.

"Hey!" he bellowed.

The men were not deterred. They did not pause or hesitate. A thought crossed my mind—I should have drawn the blinds. Then they wouldn't have known where we all were.

But they did know. One went straight for my husband, the other for me.

I grabbed the pot of boiling water and tossed it at the man in the kitchen. He screamed as it hit his chest, but my son screamed too. I'd splashed him with the water. His face was sizzling. Then I was screaming and on my knees beside the table, bringing my boy into my chest and kissing his head.

My head rattled like a gong, and my face hit the floor, shattering my front teeth and sending them across the linoleum like dropped porcelain. I rolled over and saw the man looming above me, brandishing a cast iron pan that had been hanging above the island. My vision waxed and waned, and the back of my head throbbed. My son's piercing screams made my eyes water, and I looked toward him. He was on the floor, his hands on my face, pleading with me to get up. I saw a dark movement and turned my head away. Closed my eyes. I didn't want to see.

I heard the impact as the pan struck my son. I closed my eyes tight, and tears leaked out of the corners. My son's body slumped over my chest, heaving with every strike of the pan until I could feel his little breath anymore. I wished he'd just let out one more breath. One more laugh. Maybe all I needed was a funny YouTube video ...

My son's weight was lifted, and I felt rough hands tearing at my dress. I struggled, and the pan slammed on the side of my head. I punched and he punched back. I bit and he bit a chunk out of my cheek. My body was screaming, but my lungs were quiet. I struggled until I couldn't, and even then, I wriggled and writhed, even as my clothes were tossed to the side and the cold floor was pressed against my back.

When he forced himself inside me, I stopped moving. I didn't want to aid in his pleasure. I stayed very still as he jackhammered me, tearing me, grunting and drooling over my bare breasts and face. I turned my head to the side to avoid his rank breath, and my eyes came open. I wished they hadn't.

I saw movement. My husband was struggling with the other man, but the other man was larger, wider, taller. I blinked. A long, dark pause. When I opened my eyes, my husband was on his knees, hands up, a gun pressed into the back of his head.

I closed my eyes.

BANG.

I opened my eyes. My husband was on the floor, his face turned toward me. But it wasn't his face. It was ground meat.

I closed my eyes. Heard a soft cry.

I opened my eyes. There was a woman hovering over my husband, touching his face, trying to shake him awake. She was lovely. In her twenties, dusty golden ringlets just like my daughter has, and a birthmark on her forearm, just like my daughter. The woman was wearing a wedding dress, a masterpiece of lace and embroidery and quiet ivory. Exactly the fairy-tale dress my daughter would have worn.

I blinked. Long and slow. Opened my eyes.

It was not a bride over my husband. It was my daughter. She was crying, calling for her daddy, for me, touching what was left of his face.

I closed my eyes.

BANG.

My daughter was no more. I opened my eyes and saw a blood-soaked wedding dress draped over my husband like a funeral shroud.

"You just about done?" my daughter's murderer asked his friend.

Oh right. I was being raped.

One last, deep thrust and I felt my son's murdered come inside me, the fluid pooling beneath my ass as he pulled out his deflating cock.

They were laughing. Their speech was a jumbled mess in my head.

" *... my turn ... but Imma go in the backdoor ... don't want your spunk on my junk ...*"

I heard boots coming toward me. I looked to the living room, avoiding the bloody mess on the floor, and saw a flurry of movement.

NO!

My daughter's murderer was coming to sodomize me. And he would have already reached me if it wasn't for the puppies jumping at his legs and tugging at his laces.

NO!

They were licking him, pouncing, wanting to play.

"Fucking mutts!" he yelled.

I didn't look away in time. He lifted his boot and stomped, crushing the skull of the first puppy with a sickening squelch. He giggled, then went for the next.

I closed my eyes.

My body was broken and exhausted. I wanted to lift my hand and cover my ears, but I was too groggy to move. I was quite certain there was blood sloshing around my brain, and I wished I would just die.

Another stomp, and the splintering of bones.

Stomp, a tiny yelp, and the sound of footsteps in a wet garden.

Stomp, yelp, squelch.

Six times. Six deaths.

I barely felt it when he rolled me over and pulled me up on my knees. My husband and I had never done this, so it would be nice and tight for him. Maybe he'd be happy, and he'd leave, and time would reset, and everything would be okay.

But it wasn't. I ripped, I screamed, my insides prolapsed to the outside, and I closed my eyes.

After the rapes were done and all but my murder complete, I'd played dead. Good ole, stiff ole possum. They laughed, they joked, they cleaned themselves up in my kitchen sink that was full of sippy cups and coffee mugs. They chatted, all nonchalant, as they scoured my house for valuables. Once both men were upstairs, I struggled to my hands and knees and crawled over the field of slaughtered pups to the basement door. I opened it silently—not that it mattered, they wouldn't have heard anything over the racket they were making upstairs.

When I hit the carpet at the bottom of the stairs, I ran to the spare bedroom. I threw the door open to find Juno frantic, with wood shavings on the inside of the door from her trying to claw her way out.

"How'd you get locked in here?" I asked.

I was thrilled she had. I grabbed her, pulled her into the closet, and closed the door.

THEY ARE GOING to find us. I have blood pouring from all my orifices. Surely, I left a trail.

They will come, and they will kill me.

And they will find Juno.

"Oh, girl," I say, and I hug her.

Juno is it. All I have left. She's been my rock, my heart, my love through all the times.

Juno whimpers. She doesn't know what she's lost.

A voice comes from upstairs, sing-song and taunting.

"We playing hide and seek, honey? We thought you was a goner! Seems you gots some life in you yet."

Dogs are resilient. Juno's not that old. Only a year older than my son is.

Was.

She'll make someone an excellent companion.

"They don't know," I say. "They don't know about you."

"Gotta go, sweetheart!" the other man calls. *"Can't leave you alive to tattle now, can we?"*

Juno's fur glimmers silver in the dark. Her eyes are wet with fear but warm with love. I kiss her forehead, remembering all the kisses I'd left there. I remember all the times she saved me.

"My turn to save you, girl."

I hug Juno, then struggled to my feet. She licks me.

"Stay," I say as I cover her in her yellow blanket. "Stay quiet."

I kiss her on the forehead. I leave the closet, closing the door behind me.

Her fur on my lips is the last thing I feel.

Jae Mazer is a Canadian who was born in Victoria, British Columbia, and grew up in the prairies of Northern Alberta. After spending the majority of her life battling sasquatches in the Great White North, she migrated south to Texas to have a go at the armadillos. She is a connoisseur and creator of gothic horror, splatterfolk, splatter westerns, and folk horror. She's degreed, won awards, been in anthologies, owns a couple of breweries, has chameleon hair and lots of skin ink, and enjoys mustard and alcohol.

GRETEL

(A GRANDPAPPY STORY)

PATRICK C. HARRISON III

He'd killed her ninety-three times now, if his count was accurate. Maybe more if one or more of his many blackout-drunk rages involved mangy elderly mut execution. Make that *attempted* execution. Because there she sat on the weathered living room rug, staring up at Al and wagging her goddamn tail like she had something a hell of a lot tastier than a swift leather boot to the teeth coming her way.

"Scram, you little shit," Al said, kicking his pointed boot out at the dog. From his spot in the old recliner, which sagged inward with age, he couldn't quite reach her.

The dog took one startled step away from the kick, then settled onto her ass again, her tail flicking about happily, her tongue lolling to one side. Gretel was an old beagle, graying around her muzzle, and thinner than a young, strong pup. She was sixteen or seventeen, Al figured, so getting on in years, ready for the goddamn grave.

"If she would stay in that goddamn grave," Al muttered as he brought a cigarette to his lips. Taking a gas station lighter out of the pocket of his worn, faded Dickies, he eyed the dog again.

"Fuck you," he said as his cigarette came to life. He inhaled and exhaled then watched a western on the television for a time, as a cold winter wind moaned and whined, causing the old bones of the house to protest in creaky fashion. The gleam of the TV reflected on Gretel's lifeless, watching eyes, and Al couldn't help but nervously meet her gaze ever so often.

She was barely more than a pup the first time he killed her. It wasn't even entirely purposeful on Al's part. There was a Hansel to go along with Gretel back in those days. Though they were named after the popular fairy tale siblings, the dogs were not, in fact, brother and sister. Hansel was a pug and about six months older than Gretel.

Al and his wife, Marjorie, had bought both of them at a flea market outside Fort Worth. It was a spur-of-the-moment acquisition, a purchase made when their bellies were full of roasted turkey leg and funnel cakes, and their minds were full of the haze brought on by marijuana cigarettes and Oxycontin. Al and Marjorie were in good spirits, in other words, and had even engaged in a bout of raucous sex the night before, even though they were well into their fifties at the time.

So buying not just one but two pups seemed like an idea of grand breadth. And the young Mexican boy was selling them for only twenty bucks a pup out of the back of a dusty pickup, so what the hell, right? Except all good buzzes come to an end, and more often than not that dissipating buzz comes with a price to pay. Typically, that materializes in little more than an annoying headache and perhaps a nice case of the liquid shits.

But when Al and Marjorie emerged tiresomely from their trip down euphoria lane, they were greeted not by headaches or any other physical ailments (they were, by this time, pros in the ways of booze and bud and pills alike, thus weren't prone to such things), but by a pug that shit on the floor and humped at one's leg and a beagle that yapped at every sound and sniffed at damn near everything.

It took Al all of about thirty minutes upon their arrival home to realize the mistake he'd made. No dog food or dog bowls or dog pens or dog anything had been purchased. Before the first evening had drawn to a close, he'd already cursed at the dogs a dozen times, thrown a few crumpled beer cans at them, kicked Hansel off his leg, thrown Gretel into the backyard for yapping too much, and yelled at Marjorie for not cleaning the shit off the rug quick enough. All the same, he didn't kill Gretel on purpose the first time.

The first time came just a few months after they'd purchased the dogs. They were still plenty young but neither Hansel nor Gretel could really be called puppies anymore. Marjorie, for some goddamn reason, had by this point taken a real liking to Gretel, despite her constant barking and howling and sniffing at every fucking thing. And despite the fact she'd taken to digging holes in the backyard every time Al threw her back there for any extended period.

Thus, Marjorie was insistent on having Gretel involved in anything her and Al did. She wanted Gretel sitting on the couch beside her when they watched *Gunsmoke*. She wanted Gretel tagging along when they went for a walk or went fishing or went to visit their daughter Monica and her new baby Charles. And, of course, she wanted Gretel involved in bedroom activities.

Oh, it wasn't as if there was any pooch pussy penetration going on. Al had no desire to attempt cramming his cock into the tiny hole of a frantic, clawing mut, and Marjorie didn't fancy fingerbanging a dog's browneye or anything like that. But it wasn't a canine cuckery going on either; it wasn't like Gretel just got to sit there and watch.

Al was never one for eating at the Y. Not exactly a fan of

tasting hair pie or licking the lower lips. He didn't partake of sushi, tuna tacos, and certainly not the bearded clam. He didn't like eating pussy, in other words. Gretel, on the other hand, was a wonder in the ways of the tongue, if given a good reason to start lapping.

Al and Marjorie weren't every night-bangers like they used to be. As stated previously, they were in their fifties, so they partook in the horizontal rumba only once every couple of weeks or so. As Al got older, he leaned into the sadistic qualities of his erotic inspiration. He needed to inflict a little pain to get the lead in his pencil. But even though there was a pair of vice grips involved in their shenanigans, it wasn't Al's kink that killed Gretel.

The first couple of times they banged with the dog in the bed, Marjorie used whipped cream. She slapped that mess between her legs and up her ass crack and then along her inner thighs. She was a hefty, sagging woman, having lost any firmness to her body to the annals of time, and Al was of the opinion the whipped cream between her tree trunk thighs looked like a goddamn yeast infection bubbling out of her twat. There wasn't enough stolen cash in the pockets of Congress to get him kneeling down there with his tongue ready to work.

Gretel was another story, though. She'd lap that shit up like it was both her first *and* last meal at the same. That bitch, with her tail wagging so fast Al thought she might go floating into the air like a helicopter, ingested the whipped cream so fast, you'd think a timer had been set to it, like an Olympic gold medal was at stake.

Marjorie, naturally, squealed like a newborn pig with a razor in its gut. Only, in a more delighted fashion. The problem, however, was Gretel was too damn fast. A little lick, lap, and the fluttering of a tail, and Marjorie's cocksleeve was cream free, leaving only her wrinkled folds and gray pubes and a couple of moles and an odor that had always been a mite sour.

She'd go to whining about not having her cooter ate out while Al ran sewing needles through her saggy tits or put cigarettes out on her skintags or some such fun. She didn't enjoy his sadistic qualities near as much if she didn't have that dog's tongue going to town on her fajita meat.

Thus, it was Al's brilliant idea to slap peanut butter between her legs. Two whole handfuls, in fact. One handful damn near stopped up her honey hole and the other was smeared generously all along her ass crack, which was longer than the normal ass crack, Al had always thought. His thinking was simple: peanut butter was thicker, stickier, and difficult as hell to eat quickly, which in theory would result in Gretel going down on Marjorie for a hell of a lot longer, so Al could focus on face-fucking his wife while sprinkling cayenne pepper in her nose and eyes and twisting her ear with a pair of vice grips.

Only, it turned out Gretel was allergic to peanut butter.

Al had finally managed to get Marjorie's dentures out (her hands were tied to the bedposts, so she couldn't do it herself) and was sliding his tighty-whities off and kicking them off his crusty toes when the woman started whining about Gretel not lapping on her hoo-ha anymore. Sure enough, the bitch was laying on her side between Marjorie's legs wheezing like a whistle with every gasping breath.

Marjorie, of course, panicked and wanted Al to rush the dog to the vet, where they could give her an epinephrine shot or steroids or whatever helped an allergic reaction. Because Gretel's neck was swelling up to where it didn't look like she even had a neck. Marjorie, having ripped her way out of her restraints, was screaming for Al to get her to the local doggy ER.

Al wasn't having it, though. He wasn't gonna pay out the ass to save some little bitch dog he picked up at a flea market. Fuck that. She ruined his night of romance and he was supposed to rush her off to some vet where they would demand untold fortunes just to save a dog? Fuck no. All Al intended to do for Gretel was help her into the wastebasket, which was exactly what he did eventually.

First though, because Marjorie wouldn't shut the hell up, he pulled out his pocket knife and cut a hole in Gretel's throat and shoved a straw into the hole. But the makeshift trach only made matters worse, causing the damned pup to cough up blood and wheeze it back into her lungs.

So Gretel died that night. For goddamn sure, Gretel died. Al wrapped her in three Kmart plastic bags and threw her ass into the kitchen trashcan. Then, with Marjorie in hysterics again, he took the bagged-up pooch from the trash and buried her about a foot deep in the backyard. Marjorie said a prayer over her grave. It was the first time he'd ever heard her pray and the only time he ever would.

Yet the next morning, as Al crawled out of bed and hobbled toward the bathroom for his first whiz of the day, he heard a faint scratching at the backdoor. As he emerged from the pisser, tucking his dick back in his briefs and shaking a few drops of urine from his fingertips, the sound of scratching intensified, and goddamn Hansel started barking at the door.

In nothing but his tighty whities and a loose-fitting wifebeater, Al paced to the back of the house, lit a cigarette, and angrily flung the door open.

And there stood Gretel on the back step, wagging her tail and looking happily up at Al as if they were best pals.

"You gotta be fuckin' shittin' me," was what Al managed to say, staring dumbly down at the mut, his cigarette teetering on the edge of his lip.

Gretel waltzed right into the house like she owned the damn place, passing by Hansel and passing by a bowl of dog food too, heading straight for the master bedroom, where she yapped Marjorie awake. Marjorie was overjoyed and said it was a miracle and all this and that. Al huffed and cursed under his breath and was perplexed about the whole situation.

Every other time, she was killed on purpose.

One evening, Gretel wouldn't stop barking at the front door, so Al, screaming through a cloud of smoke and whiskey breath, opened the door slightly, held the dog in between it and the doorjamb, and slammed the door into the dog's body thirteen times, breaking ribs and crushing her insides. Blood poured from her mouth, nose, and ass by the time he was done. Gretel was dead and in the wastebasket. And then an hour or so later she was crawling her ass out of the trash with barbeque sauce from Al's discarded dinner matting her fur.

On a summer morning not long after that, Al tripped over Gretel and stubbed his toe on the end table, which lead to Al angrily hefting the dog into the air and slamming her on the wood floor half a dozen times, cursing and red-faced the whole time. When he stopped, with Marjorie wailing behind him, Gretel was broken and bleeding. One rib was sticking out of her left side looking like the sharp barb of a catfish. Her front right leg was bent four different directions. She stopped breathing as Marjorie pounded her balled fists on Al's chest, screaming about what an asshole he was.

Al took dead Gretel by the tale and tossed her in the backyard, not bothering to bag or bury her this time, because he had an inkling she wasn't completely done living yet. And he was right—she was scratching at the backdoor an hour or so later.

The next time, about month after Hansel met his own fiery demise (as it turned out, Hansel did not have the same return-from-the-grave attribute as Gretel), Al shot Gretel in the back-yard with a pre-64 Winchester 30-30, which his neighbor was trying to sell to Al so he could pay for a divorce lawyer. The rifle, which Al did not end up buying, killed Gretel for certain. The bullet went in one side of her torso and blew her guts out the other. Yet the next morning she was ready and waiting for her morning helping of Alpo.

After that, it became a bit of a sport to kill Gretel anytime Al got a hankering for violence, and violence was always a substantial slice of his disposition pie chart. Marjorie, who protested mightily the first few times Gretel met the reaper, became indifferent to the dog's various deaths. She even killed her herself a couple of times, once when she wouldn't stop barking at something in the yard in the middle of the night and once when Gretel snatched a large piece of meatloaf off Marjorie's plate when she sat it on the end table in the living room. Both times, Marjorie stabbed the pooch with a steak knife.

Al was much more creative in his means of killing Gretel.

Once, he broke Gretel's legs so she couldn't get away, slathered her in grape jelly, and tossed her atop angry ant bed.

Another time, he opened her belly up with a fillet knife, took hold of a length of her intestines, and swung her around his head in the backyard like a lasso.

He forced gasoline down her gullet and then shot her with a flaming arrow—KABOOM!

He chopped Gretel to pieces with an eight-pound axe. Within minutes, the pieces of doggo meat were pulling themselves back together again.

No matter what Al did, Gretel would return within a day, sometimes looking a little worn out but still breathing and wagging her goddamn tail. Al didn't have a clue what kind of sorcery was at play here, nor did he much care. He didn't ponder on the *why*, for it wasn't in his nature to ponder on such things. But after nearly two decades, he'd grown plenty tired of dealing with Gretel. He never really wanted the dog to begin with.

Now, with Marjorie six months in the grave after dying from an aggressive case of cunt cancer, Al wanted to get rid of the damned mut once and for all, because he was sick of having to let her outside to piss and buy her food and share the goddamn couch with her. There was something sickly about her, like she was rotten even though she was alive and well. She had a funk about her. Her coat, silky smooth when they first bought her, was prickly in a way, and the flesh beneath was mushy and lumpy, like she was filled with cold oatmeal. All the dying and coming back to life had changed Gretel.

And dropping her off in the middle of nowhere apparently wasn't an option either. Like some Looney Tunes gag, if Al tossed Gretel out the car window while doing eighty on the interstate three hours from home, Gretel would be scratching at the back door the next morning. Al knew this because he'd tried it. Once, he'd thrown Gretel in the lake with a cinderblock chained to her hindlegs, and damned if that fucker didn't beat Al back to the house. She was drinking pissy water from the toilet bowl when he got there.

But he could get rid of her for a little while. Several hours for sure and as much as a day. Al was fairly certain the longest she'd ever stayed gone was when he cooked her to a crisp in the deep fryer. She was gone almost an entire twenty-four hours that time. Perhaps, he thought, it was the heat that kept her. But he didn't ponder on it long, being as that wasn't in his nature. His mind was made up—he'd cook the shit out of her.

"Fuckin' dog," Al said, sucking on the last of his cigarette.

On cue, Gretel leaped from the floor onto the couch beside him, as if he'd beckoned for her company.

"Get down, you stinky little shit!" he screamed, shoving Gretel to the floor where she thudded painfully. "I told you a thousand times to stay off the goddamn couch!" Stubbing his cigarette out in the ashtray, he leaned over and grabbed Gretel by the neck, lifting her as he stood, his old knees creaking. "Time to bake a little beagle pie, you old bag of bones!"

He walked to the kitchen carrying Gretel away from his body like a sack of dirty diapers. Once there, using his other hand he grabbed the blender from the cupboard, a model Marjorie bought not long after their honeymoon, fifty-plus years ago. Al never was a man who knew his away about the kitchen, but he knew they didn't make blenders like this anymore, that would last half a century and turn granite to dust. Gretel, though thinner and mushier than she once was, would be tough to fit into the blender. But Al reckoned he'd give it the ol' college try.

After plugging it in and flipping off the plastic lid, he turned the blades on high and it whirred to life, sounding not unlike a miniature airplane.

"Ready to go for a little spin, bitch?" Al said, bringing Gretel close to his face.

She responded by licking his nose, as if he were offering her a pup cup at the coffee chop drive thru.

"God damn you!"

So in Gretel went, face first. The blades of the blender mowed through her snout. Almost instantly there were chunks of furry flesh and broken teeth spinning about within the glass. She actually tried to bark once and the noise came out reminiscent of how it sounds to speak through a fan. This made Al smile as he force fed his dog down further.

The skull was tough. Al had to pull Gretel back several times to allow the blades to start whirring at full speed again. Eventually, with Al pushing down more slowly, Gretel's orange-sized head was shaving apart piece by piece, with bone, brain, and blood joining the ever-expanding broth within the blender. Even so, he couldn't get Gretel all the way blended. He got all of her head and about half of her torso whipped into a pink, soupy mixture. But her hindlegs were still pointed into the air and her tail was draped over the side of the blender like a lifeless snake.

Al thought about flipping the pooch around and blending the rest but ultimately decided to just dump the whole mess into the roasting pan and get on with it. He set the oven to bake at 450 and dumped the Gretel sludge into the deep roasting pan, something that he hadn't used since a Thanksgiving he could no longer recall.

Sliding the pan in and closing the oven, he set the timer to sixty minutes then grabbed himself a Keystone from the fridge, opening it and drinking half the contents before arriving back at the couch. Then Al put *Big Jake* in the VCR and lit up a cigarette and forgot about that damn dog. It was an hour of bliss if there ever was one. There weren't many things better than cheap smokes and cheap beer, combined with an empty house so he could watch the Duke in peace.

He was five beers and six cigarettes deep when the oven timer went off. Al was lost in the old west, having almost forgotten that stupid mut even existed until the bell rang. When the timer dinged, he was surprised by not having smelled the doggo slop cooking. Hell, at 450 degrees Gretel should have been bubbling over the side of the pan and burning to a crisp at the bottom of the oven. As it was, he didn't smell a goddamn thing.

Taking a drag on his cigarette and placing the still smoking butt in the ashtray, Al got up with a groan and headed for the kitchen without giving the lack of smell much thought. It wasn't in his nature, after all. He figured once he pulled Gretel from the oven he'd dump the slop in the backyard. Maybe he'd even squirt the mess with lighter fluid and set it ablaze. For all he knew a little bit of overkill might give him an entire day without the mut.

Al opened the drawer next to the stove and retrieved a pair of oven mitts Marjorie made some twenty years ago. He slid them on and flung open the oven, squinting at the heat. And there the pan was...empty. Gretel and the chunky, runny chowder she'd become was gone.

He stared into the heat, confused, for a moment or two. Grabbing the pan, which felt feather light in his hands, he set it on the stovetop, then looked again into the open mouth of the oven, as if the bitch might come bounding out of there with her tail wagging. But there was no dog, burnt up or otherwise. So he closed the door and turned the oven off and returned the mitts to the drawer.

Giving the empty pan a curious glance, Al got another Keystone from the fridge and walked slowly back to the living room, where he plopped back down on the couch and placed the cigarette back where it belonged. He smoked it down and took a long, refreshing drink of his beer. *Big Jake* continued on the television but he wasn't paying it too much mind.

Gretel had never done anything like this, disappearing into thin air like some magic trick. Typically, Al could see the dead remains of his dog, sometimes even as she put herself back together. But she'd never just disappeared. It was odd. Al turned around in the couch and eyed the piece of the oven he could see from this perspective. For once he was pondering the situation.

Maybe he'd finally killed the goddamn thing. Maybe that's exactly what happened when the thing called Gretel—whatever the hell she really was—was slain beyond resurrection. When she met her last death, this mythical beast of burden simply and quietly evaporated into the ether, like she was never there at all.

This thought brought a rattling chuckle out of Al, followed by a worrisome bout of coughing. Taking another cigarette from the pack, he fired it up and returned his eyes to the movie. If Gretel was gone, that would be a blessing of immeasurable proportions. If she wasn't, oh the fuck well. He'd dealt with her furry ass for years and he could put up with her for a few more, at least until the goddamn cancer sticks ushered him to his grave. Al sighed relief as he smoked.

The Duke was in the midst of a gunfight when something small fell in front of the television, splatting on the wood floor. It had come from up high, falling from the ceiling, Al thought. But what the hell would fall from up there? A bug of some kind?

"The fuck was that?" Al said, snatching up the VCR remote and hitting pause on a scene of John Wayne blasting his revolver.

He looked at the floor in front of the TV, squinting. It was some kind of black, oily sludge, not much bigger than those big cockroaches that came around in the spring months. Al crinkled his nose and looked up to the ceiling above the spot on the floor. It was cracked from foundation issues and discolored from years of cigarette smoke but he didn't see anything wet and leaking. Did he have any anything up in that area of the attic? Al couldn't remember—he hadn't been up there in years—but he didn't think so.

Looking back down at the floor, he leaned forward, readying himself to get up and take a closer look, when there was a splat just inches from his right boot. Black goo, the glow of the television gleaming on its surface. It looked like a spatter of blood a little smaller than Al's hand, except black instead of red, and thicker in consistency.

"What the goddamn hell?"

Al looked up again, this time seeing pieces of the ceiling or the paint of the ceiling dripping down like fat water droplets, instantly turning oily black the second it left the surface. It rained down between him and the TV, splatting all over the wood floorboard and the old rug that ran across there. Al watched it accumulate with wild, confused eyes.

Then he noticed, too, the globules of black slime were coming *out* of the wood and *out* of the rug. Not emerging from between the cracks of the boards or tears in the carpet, but emerging off of the floor and ceiling as if it had always been a part of it. And, gawking now, Al looked around himself and saw the stuff coming off the couch. Again, not bleeding from the fabric as if it were saturated, coming directly from it, as if it were hidden in plain sight by some perplexing biological camouflage.

Biological, yes, because the black shit wasn't stationary. It was, to Al's great astonishment, moving. All of the sludge appeared to be converging slowly, each individual globe sliding silently toward the center of the living room, right between the television and Al's spot on the couch.

As each piece joined it made a certain *bloop* sound, like a drippy faucet delivering another drop to an already-full bowl of water. Each splat brought itself together and headed in that same central direction, looking like an army of fat, black ants converging. Until there were no more splats or globs or oily slugs left. Only a large black pillow of the substance, reminiscent of the round loaves of bread Al's mother used to bake.

He simply looked on in ever more bewildering horror. His cigarette teetered forgotten on his lower lip. His boney hands were curled into nervous fists.

And then the round blob of black began to change shape, growing in height and losing some of its pudginess. It gained texture, becoming less smooth, showing bristles and appendages and a quivering kind of body, all still oily black. But Al could see now—he could see Gretel forming from this black mass of terror.

She was there, every bone, muscle, and hair of her. It was Gretel, sure as she ever was. And the blackness was giving way to her normal mixture of white, brown, and black, with a healthy helping of old dog gray. She was wagging her tail now, with her tongue hanging out. She was staring Al straight in the eyes.

"Jesus fuckin' Christ," he said, and the cigarette finally lost the battle and fell to the floor.

With that, Gretel took a couple of steps and lept upon the couch, laying her head on Al's leg. He gasped at the touch of her and started to scoot away. But the dog looked up at him, her eyes suddenly turning oily black.

Were those eyes evil?

How could they not be?

"What the fuckin' hell are you?" Al said. He slowly settled back into the couch and brought his hand down gently on Gretel's back, petting her. Al sighed nervousness and the dog sighed too.

loving, loyal doggo—Nora.

Patrick C. Harrison III (PC3, if you prefer) is an author of horror, splatterpunk, and all forms of speculative fiction. His works include 100% Match, Grandpappy, and Queen Boss Slay, and his short stories can be found in numerous anthologies and collections. PC3 lives in Wolfe City, Texas with his family and their

NIGHT OF THE NAGUAL

ROWLAND BERCY JR.

Chapter 1

From a young age, Leroy sensed he was different. His abuela, Claudia, who devoted her life to studying the spiritual beliefs of their ancestors, was confident Leroy's date of birth indicated he would become a powerful nagual—a person with the ability to shapeshift into their spiritual, or tonal, animal counterpart.

Leroy did not put much stock into the shapeshifting folklore of his Mesoamerican elders who had begun referring to him in hushed tones as "brujo," a term of reverence amongst his people synonymous with magic. While he was convinced the shapeshifting rumors were complete rubbish, he was a firm believer that one could gain strength and spiritual wisdom through a connection through their tonal animal, a notion which proved true after he acquired his tonal, Luna, a fiercely loyal Dobermann Pinscher. Their connection was immediate and Leroy knew, without a doubt, she would be the catalyst by which he could delve deeper into his craft.

"Mark my words, mijo. Now that you're coupled with Luna, it's only a matter of time until you manifest the full potential of your powers," Claudia repeated, for what had to be the hundredth time, as they sat down for their Saturday morning breakfast. Leroy and Claudia had a special connection made stronger from her years of mentoring him. "Have you contemplated further on your shifter capabilities?"

"Grandma, there's no such thing as shapeshifting. The legends you've told me of naguals able to morph into their animal counterparts are nothing more than old wives' tales. Luna has without a doubt increased my gifts since our union-- haven't you girl," he said reaching down to scratch his faithful companion, who was never far from his side, behind her ears. She immediately sat up straighter and leaned into Leroy's affections as he continued. "But not once have I felt the slightest inkling of these so-called changeling abilities. If there is such a thing as shapeshifting, why haven't you taken the form of Azul, and taken flight to soar across the skies?" Leroy asked, inciting an indignant squawk of protest from the stunning Blue Macaw perched on the back of his grandmother's chair.

Claudia shook her head and smiled at Leroy's inexperience. "Shifting takes on many different definitions when it comes to nagual's and their tonal companions. While it's true that the tonal will always strengthen a nagual's psychic prowess, in various, and unexpected ways, unfortunately, not every nagual is endowed with the capacity to shift."

Leroy grinned as he grabbed a crunchy strip of bacon from his plate and presented it to Luna. The rest of the meal passed quickly as he and Claudia chatted contentedly.

"So, what sort of mischief do you have planned for the remainder of the day?" she queried.

Leroy smiled dreamingly.

"So, you're seeing Jae later, huh?" she asked when the look of elation illuminated her grandson's face.

"Yeah. I have a few errands to run, then I'll be meeting up with Jae at the dog park. After that, we'll probably grab a bite to eat then catch a late movie."

Leroy and Jae, who was well aware of Leroy's Nagual capabilities, had been dating for three years and things were going great. So great, Leroy planned to ask Jae to marry him. He already had the perfect ring, which he carried with him at all times, waiting for the right moment to pop the question.

"Well, you boys have a great day, but please be aware of your surroundings," Claudia said, her voice laced with concern. "The streets around here aren't what they used to be."

"Will do," Leroy promised as he stood up from the table. He grabbed their breakfast plates and took them to the kitchen to be washed before leaving for the day.

"Go on, now. I'll take care of the mess later," Claudia said, standing to see her grandson off.

Startled by the sudden movement, Azul flapped off her chair and took flight, squawking noisily as he circled the room.

Claudia rolled her eyes at the antics of her tonal and smiled.

Leroy set the plates in the sink and walked over to his grandmother and embraced her. "I love you, grandma."

"I love you too, now scram," Claudia responded affectionately. "And take that mangy mutt with you while you're at it," she continued with a wink and a smile.

Luna, who was playfully chasing Azul around the room, stopped and looked at Claudia with prideful displeasure at the audacity of being called 'mangy.'

"Come on Luna, let's go. It's clear that we're not wanted here" Leroy joked as he made his way out the door into the temperate morning air.

. . .

Chapter 2

LEROY LOUNGED on a bench in the dog park, enjoying the warm rays of sun on his face as Luna frolicked around enthusiastically. The sight of his beloved tonal disappearing behind a small row of hedges caused him an irrational moment of fear, for he couldn't bear the thought of life without her. Their connection was so deep, Luna sensed his distress and worriedly popped her head up from behind the bush to make sure he was all right. Secure in the knowledge that all was well, Luna went back to doing what dogs do best and sped off to chase a tossed tennis ball.

Leroy surrendered himself to the tranquility of the day and closed his eyes and let his mind wander. Before long, he shuddered with anticipation, which sent delightful impulses through every vein in his body as he felt a pair of hands slink across the back of his head and over his eyes. The stranger's arms pulled Leroy into an embrace. Leroy shuddered as the most incredible kisses were planted along the nape of his neck. "I don't know who you are, but my boyfriend won't be too pleased if he walks up to see a stranger kissing on me," Leroy said, trying to keep a straight face, but failing miserably as the corners of his lips betrayed his amusement.

"Well, we should probably get out of here before he arrives," a deep, seductive voice replied.

Responding to her master's enthusiasm, as easily as she did his worry, Luna abandoned her assault on the tennis ball and sprinted over to greet Jae, whom she had also developed an attachment to over the past three years.

Upon seeing the charging dog, Jae stepped back with his

hands outstretched in front of him. "Luna, wait. Luna, slow down girl. Luna! Luna! Luna!" Jae shrieked as the dog leaped onto his chest, knocking him into the grass where she proceeded to lick him with fervor. Jae attempted to push her away but couldn't stop laughing long enough to do much of anything else except cover his face.

Leroy, also laughing hysterically at the situation, stood up from the bench. With no more than a thought, he commanded Luna to heel, and she immediately ceased her assault on Jae and scampered over to Leroy's side.

Still laughing, Jae pushed up from the ground and dusted himself off.

Leroy walked over to him and, without a word, wrapped his arms around Jae to give him a proper greeting. "I've missed you."

The pair talked for hours, not noticing how quickly time had passed until Luna, who wore herself out romping around the park, sauntered over and hopped onto the bench between them.

"Well, I never," Jae muttered, feigning annoyance at the audacity of Leroy's tonal as he scooted away and crossed his arms over his chest.

Luna looked towards Jae with indifference, gave him a quick lick on the cheek as if to say, "And you never will," then turned away from him and rested her head on Leroy's lap. Leroy glanced between Luna and Jae. Took note of the wide-eyed look of surprise plastered across Jae's face, and started to chuckle. Soon enough, Jae joined in and they both erupted into fits of laughter. It was shaping up to be a great day.

When their laughter finally subsided Jae gave Luna a playful slap to the butt and stood. "I'm hungry; let's go grab a bite to eat."

Luna's ears perked up at the word 'eat' and she eagerly leapt from the bench.

The three of them hopped into Leroy's truck and drove to their favorite restaurant.

After dinner, Leroy, Jae, and Luna strolled the streets of downtown window shopping to pass the time. Whenever the couple ventured into a place of business, Luna obediently waited just outside the door for the men to return.

At a quarter to midnight, they found themselves approaching the theater. Knowing they'd be inside for at least two hours, Leroy instructed Luna to await their return. She was free to roam the streets and would know when to return as she would immediately detect Leroy's scent when he exited the theater.

"See you soon girl," Leroy said bending down to give Luna a satisfying scratch, then walked hand-in-hand with Jae into the theater to catch the midnight showing of the 1974 cult classic, *It's Alive.*

Chapter 3

SHORTLY AFTER 2 A.M., the men exited the theater chatting, and laughing excitedly. "That was epic! Did you check out the cheesy ass monster baby movie prop? I loved it!" Jae exclaimed. Leroy laughed and inconspicuously looked around for Luna who was nowhere to be seen. As they walked towards the truck, which was about six blocks away, the crowd around them began to dwindle. Immersed in their conversation, they were completely unaware of their surroundings as they turned down a dimly lit street.

A rustling from a row of hedges off to their left finally caught Jae's attention and he paused mid-sentence. "What the hell was that?"

"I'm not sure. You should check it out," Leroy replied and gently propelled Jae towards the shrubbery.

"You go check it out," Jae replied nervously, planting his feet firmly on the ground to avoid being pushed closer to whatever the hell it was.

Suddenly, the bushes shook violently. Jae's eyes widened in terror as a dark, hulking figure emerged. A spine-chilling growl filled the night as the beast lunged forward, smashing into Jae's chest, sending him and Leroy crashing to the grass.

The beast snapped, attempting to rip chunks of flesh from Jae's face.

Frightened and frantic, Jae screamed and flailed around to fend off the creature and give Leroy time to escape. His cries of terror faded when the pain of the attack never manifested. Slowly, he cracked open his eyes, expecting to see a gruesome cryptid, only to find Luna hunched over him with an amused sparkle in her eyes. The tension melted from his body instantly upon realizing he was not in danger.

Leroy laughed hysterically.

"You jerk!" Jae said, his voice filled with good-natured humor.

Luna jumped away and Jae turned over to face Leroy, who was still cackling wildly. Jae's face twisted into a sly grin as he leaned in closer. "Oh, you think that's funny, huh?" And he began tickling Leroy under his arms.

"Ok, ok. I'm sorry," Leroy said, struggling to catch his breath through the laughter.

The men gazed lovingly at each other, amusement, joy and passion gleaming in their eyes. Jae planted a tender kiss on Leroy's lips and embraced him tightly.

Leroy knew the ideal moment to ask the question had finally come.

· · ·

Chapter 4

LEROY REACHED into his pocket and was just moments away from retrieving the ring when a voice startled them.

"Great, just what this neighborhood needs. A pair of faggots' tongue wrestling on the streets. Fuckin' disgusting. What if some innocent child was to walk up and see two queers fuckin'?"

Leroy and Jae picked themselves up from the ground and stood side-by-side facing the two men who stumbled across them.

Luna moved to stand in front of them and bared her teeth threateningly to the strangers.

The men continued their advance, undaunted.

"It's two o'clock in the morning. I don't think there's much chance for any kid to walk up on us. And just for the record, we weren't fuckin'. Why am I not surprised you don't know the difference between fucking and kissing?" Jae spoke confidently, not easily intimidated.

The man narrowed his eyes menacingly at being mocked in front of his partner-in-crime and flicked out a switchblade which glinted brightly in the streetlight. "Keep runnin' that fag mouth and I swear I'll slice your fuckin' tongue off and ram it down your throat."

Seeing what could quickly escalate into a violent situation, Leroy stepped forward. "Look guys, we're not looking for any trouble."

"I suggest you shut the fuck up, brujo," the man said. "I know who you are. Heard about you and your looney ass grandma. Heard you're supposed to be able to see into the future or some shit. Guess you're not as good as the rumors say you are. You didn't see this coming, now did you?"

This time, Leroy's eyes narrowed. "It doesn't work like that, Edwin. We know who you are too. You and Edgar have been a pain in the ass ever since I can remember. Now, why don't you both politely fuck off."

"Who the fuck do you think you're talkin' to?" Edgar, Edwin's twin brother, sneered. Over his shoulder was a wooden bat inspired by Negan's Lucille from *The Walking Dead*.

Luna's hackles rose and she growled louder.

"I suggest you leash that bitch or I will bash its fuckin' head in." Edgar brandished his baseball bat as he spoke. "And after I'm done with the mutt, maybe I'll splatter your fairy brains across the ground just for the fun of it!" He pointed the end of the bat at Leroy's face for emphasis.

Enraged by the threat to Leroy, Jae leapt for the weapon, but was too slow.

Edgar yanked the bat away and swung it forward in one fluid motion.

Jae tried to evade the attack, but the bat connected with his fingertips. He shrieked in agony and hugged his injured hand close to his chest.

Luna darted between Jae and Edgar. While doing so, Edgar landed a blow to her face on his backswing. She yelped as one of her canine teeth was knocked free from her snout.

Leroy let out a pained cry and instinctively touched the side of his face as if he, too, had just been hit. "No! Luna back!" he shouted when Edwin moved in with a knife raised towards his tonal. "Go! Take Jae!"

Luna gave him a brief look before letting out a worried whine.

Leroy snapped his fingers and pointed in the direction of home. "Go now!"

The dog obeyed and turned her attention to Jae, biting into the bottom of his shirt to drag him away.

Pinned under her strong jaws, Jae fought back, eventually ripping the fabric of his shirt and freeing himself from Luna's grip.

Luna, having been given an order, wrapped her muzzle around Jae's wrist, trapping him with enough force he could not break free without harming himself. She planted all four feet firmly on the ground and dragged Jae around the corner and out of sight.

"Luna, let go!" Jae shouted, to no avail, while Leroy did all he could to distract the brothers.

"Look guys," Leroy said calmly, raising his hands in resignation, "just let us go and no one has to know about this." He was about to turn and run when Edgar, the more aggressive of the twins, took a swing at him.

Edgar's intention was a hit to Leroy's shoulder, but the bat connected with a sickening crack against the back of his head instead. The force of the impact split Leroy's skull open. He crumpled to the ground, where he lay motionless on the unforgiving surface.

"What the fuck man?" Edwin cursed angrily, snatching the bat from his brother's grip. "Why the hell did you do that?"

Edgar gazed, dumbfounded, at the expanding puddle of red liquid pooling around Leroy's head. "It wasn't intentional, man. I didn't mean to hit him so hard. All I was trying to do was give him a bit of a scare."

"Explain that shit to the police, you idiot," Edwin spat. "We gotta' get the fuck outta' here, like pronto, and we can't go back to our place."

"Where the fuck are we gonna' go then?"

"We'll go to Nana's house. The electricity is still on and nobody's been there since she passed away. I don't think anyone will look for us there."

The boys' late grandmother's house was about 10 miles from town, situated on a solitary piece of land. It sat untouched for the past year and would probably remain so until their mother decided what she wanted to do with it.

"Good idea. We can hide there until we come up with a better plan."

Chapter 5

LEROY LAY IN THE HOSPITAL, still in a coma, two weeks after the vicious blow to his skull. He was breathing on his own, a small comfort to his grandmother and Jae, who stayed by his side the whole time. The 20-plus staples, along with the abrasions on his face, were healing, though not as quickly as they would have with Luna at his side, but the hospital's no pet policy prevented that from happening.

The police hadn't been able to make any progress tracking down Leroy's assailants, even after Jae provided them with their names.

———

"I STRONGLY RECOMMEND against taking your grandson out of the hospital, Mrs. Munoz," Doctor Rubio told Claudia, who was determined to have Leroy moved back to her house where she could look after him better.

"I understand your apprehension, Doctor, but my decision is final. Leroy needs to be home where he can rest properly."

Reluctantly, Dr. Rubio relented, but insisted a medical professional come to the home several times a week to assist in Leroy's care.

Claudia, also reluctantly, agreed. Two days later, Leroy was transferred from the hospital back to his home after Claudia and Jae were instructed on how to care for him.

Luna, who had been sulking since being separated from Leroy, bound into the room and straight up onto the bed with him.

"Careful girl," Claudia said, laying a restraining hand on her.

Luna whined anxiously then settled down next to her master.

Claudia told Jae to go home to get some rest. He was about to insist he stay with Leroy, but Claudia's soft smile eased his reservations. "No need to fret. Now that Luna and Leroy are together again, everything will be alright." Claudia spoke in a soothing voice, her words radiating with comfort.

"Will you call me if he wakes while I'm away? And if he does, make sure he knows I've been here the whole time?" Jae inquired.

"I promise."

Once Jae left, Claudia returned to Leroy's bedside and swept his hair away from his temple. "You're home now, my boy, and Luna is here with you. You'll start feeling better soon."

Leroy responded with a soft moan. This was the first real verbalization since the attack.

Claudia was sure his proximity to Luna had something to do with that. She stepped back in surprise when Leroy slowly raised his arm and laid a hand atop Luna's head. Her gasp echoed throughout the room as Luna's body stiffened and shook as if she was in the throes of a seizure.

Luna's eyes suddenly emitted a ghostly amber radiance that sent chills up Claudia's spine until she realized she was witnessing Leroy's changeling abilities coming to fruition in an unexpected way. Instead of Leroy morphing into his animal counterpart, a part of his spirit was leaving his body and entering Luna.

In a matter of seconds, Luna's convulsions subsided and she sprang into a sitting position.

"Leroy? Is that you, Leroy?"

Luna's eyes lit up with understanding and she *woofed* affirmatively.

To ensure Luna's response wasn't reflexive, Claudia asked, "Can you bark three times?"

"Woof! Woof! Woof!" Luna barked.

"Do you understand me? Bark once if you can," Claudia requested.

A single *'woof'* followed.

"Are you feeling any pain?"

Two barks.

Without another word, Claudia rushed forward and hugged Luna tightly. The dog let out a yelp of pain when the hug became too intense. "Oh, I'm sorry, my love."

Luna bounded off the bed and raced to the front door, pawing at it anxiously.

"You want to go outside?" Claudia asked.

Luna replied with a single bark and Claudia strode over and unlocked the door, pushing it wide. Luna dashed out of the house.

Claudia shouted after her in concern. "Luna! I mean Leroy! Where are you going? Wait for me! I'll come with you!"

Luna spun around and let out two barks.

Claudia's steps halted. She understood only Luna and Leroy working together as a shamanistic pair could achieve what they needed to do. "Please be careful." Lines of worry etched across her forehead as she watched Luna dash away.

Chapter 6

UPON REACHING THE MAIN ROAD, Luna stopped, lifted her nose into the air and inhaled deeply. Whereas a normal dog could detect scents from as far away as 12 miles, Luna's sense of smell, with Leroy's assistance, was amplified three-fold. She had no trouble whatsoever picking up Edwin and Edgar's scents and set off to hunt them down.

Nagual and tonal arrived at the home just after sundown. After doing a bit of reconnaissance of the surrounding area, it was show time.

"What the hell was that?" Edwin muttered, reaching for the remote to lower the volume of the TV. He called out for Edgar, but there was no response. He rose from the couch and went to the window to take a look outside.

As the howling noise sounded again, sending chills along Edwin's spine, he flicked on the exterior lights of the house. His eyes widened in surprise when he saw a dog. Not just any dog, but the brujo's mutt, limping round the yard.

"Yo' bro, you're not gonna' believe it, but that fuckin' dog tracked us here," Edwin shouted to his brother.

"What?"

"The dog, it's outside!" Edwin proclaimed.

"Huh?"

"Forget it."

Making up his mind to take care of the problem alone, Edwin grabbed the bat, which was propped against the entranceway, and went to confront the pesky animal. Raising the weapon above his shoulder, he approached Luna, who cowered and cried pitifully. "Stupid fuckin' mongrel," he muttered as he swung the bat at Luna's head. She unexpectedly lunged forward with a ferocious growl. Edwin yelped in shock and brought the bat down on her back instead.

The dog whimpered in pain but kept going, barreling into Edwin and sending him tumbling to the ground.

IN THE BEDROOM ACROSS TOWN, Leroy squirmed in pain as he felt Luna's injuries on his own body. His groans of discomfort echoed through the room.

Claudia took his hand in hers, her expression full of concern.

CAUGHT off guard by the sudden attack, Edwin tried to fend off the animal as best he could with the bat.

Unable to reach his face, Luna buried her canine teeth deep into Edwin's knuckles.

He screamed as a steady flow of blood gushed from the wound and the bat slipped from his grasp.

With no barrier between them, Luna clamped down on Edwin's bloody hand and shook her head violently.

His cries increased in volume. With no other course of action, he lifted his head and clamped down on Luna's muzzle with his teeth.

The canine yelped in pain and jerked away from Edwin's

crushing jaws, tearing his ring and pinky fingers off in the process.

LEROY FLAILED and writhed as a crescent-shaped bite mark appeared on the side of his face.

Claudia let out a gasp and began to pray fervently.

EDWIN CLUTCHED his mangled hand to his chest and retrieved the bat. He frantically searched for the menacing mongrel, but Luna had darted off into the darkness and was nowhere to be found. Unable to discern the creature's whereabouts, severely wounded, and obviously outmatched, Edwin stumbled back towards the house.

He made it as far as the entrance when Luna jumped onto his back with such force that his face smashed against the door. The crunch of breaking bones echoed through the air as Edwin's nose shattered upon impact. Blood spurted from his nostrils, splattering against the frame and dripping down onto the ground below. Dazed and disoriented, Edwin collapsed to the ground, feeling waves of excruciating pain shoot through his body. Luna's sharp teeth sank into his flesh, tearing chunks from his neck and scalp in a frenzy. He howled in agony, desperately thrashing and writhing in an attempt to break free from her relentless attack.

Luna's primal strength and savagery overwhelmed his slowly weakening body. Her sharp claws pierced through the skin on his back as they raked down his shoulders to his buttocks, tearing chunks of meat and sinew with each swipe. His cries were abruptly silenced by shock as he feebly raised his mangled arm towards the door knob that seemed impossibly far away.

With a fierce snarl, Luna lunged forward and clamped her razor-sharp teeth tightly around Edwin's wrist. She pulled back with all of her strength, hearing a satisfying snap as his shoulder dislocated and his arm fell limply onto his back. But Luna didn't stop there. With a frenzied determination, she tore off large chunks of flesh and scattered them unceremoniously around the porch, reveling in the hunt like a wild predator playing with its prey. The sickening crunch of bones and the metallic tang of blood filled the air as Luna savored her kill.

Chapter 7

"WHAT THE FUCK are you doing out there, bro?" Edgar asked as he stepped out of the shower, having missed all the commotion. He walked into and scanned the living room. His brother wasn't there, and the TV was switched off. Edgar looked for Edwin, room by room, but came up empty, so he walked over to the front door, grabbed hold of the handle, and swung it open.

Luna immediately pounced on him. He was knocked to the floor where he sat staring at the macabre sight of blood oozing in a steady stream from the porch overhang and trailing down the door. His heart raced, and his eyes went wild with fear as he spotted his brother's dismembered body on the ground behind the dog, which he recognized as the same mangy mutt that belonged to the man they accosted weeks ago. The gaping wounds, broken bones, and chunks of flesh missing from his brother's partly eaten body painted a grisly scene that was sure to haunt Edgar for the rest of his life.

He scuttled backward towards the kitchen, hoping to find something he could use against Luna.

Blood trickled from her jaw and a menacing growl echoed from her throat as she lunged forward without warning at Edgar's foot, and her sharp fangs punctured his heel.

In return, Edgar kicked blindly with his other foot. It connected with Luna's nose and she let out a yelp of pain but held on tenaciously, shaking her head vigorously back and forth.

A DELUGE of blood gushed unexpectedly from Leroy's nose, staining his shirt a deep crimson.

Fast as she could, Claudia grabbed a towel and frantically tried to stop the bleeding. Worry clouded her face as her grandson's condition worsened.

RAGE AND TERROR DRIVING HIM, Edgar dragged Luna, her teeth still firmly embedded in his foot, into the kitchen. Flesh tore away under her grip as he pulled her closer to the counter. He reached up, grabbed the handle of a drawer, and yanked it out, narrowly avoiding being speared by an 8-inch stainless steel knife as utensils clattered to the floor around him.

As Edgar frantically searched for a weapon, Luna let go of his ankle and scrambled up his body. She sunk her fangs into his stomach, eliciting an agonizing scream. He finally located a kitchen knife and closed his hand around the hilt, then swung it in a wide arc, burying it deep in Luna's side.

The canine yelped in pain and shook her head with one final flash of ferocity. Pointed teeth ripped through flesh with ease as

Luna fled from the wickedly sharp blade Edgar withdrew from her body, which he now held poised for another strike. She ripped a chunk of meat from his side as she evaded the incoming attack.

Edgar's heart raced as he watched a pinkish, serpentine-like creature slither after her, leaving behind a disgusting trail of blood and muddy brown residue.

Despite her own grave injuries, Luna fiercely shook the snake thing that was trapped between her powerful jaws back and forth like her favorite chew toy.

Edgar's mind struggled to grasp the gruesome reality before him. His own bowels, once safely nestled inside his body, now lay ripped free by Luna's savage attack. The metallic tang of blood filled his nostrils as he tried to contain the primal screams that tore through his throat at the sight of his mangled intestines.

Gripping his entrails in a desperate attempt to keep them from being devoured by Luna's sharp, snapping jaws, Edgar's body convulsed with pain. The slick, slippery guts slid through his fingers as he fought with all his remaining strength. The flesh tore and ripped as the pair struggled, the visceral string of innards caught in a disgusting tug-of-war began to fray. Suddenly, with a moist, sickening snap, it broke apart, showering Edgar in a gruesome spray of steaming blood, chunks of half-digested food, and excrement.

HAVING SWALLOWED the last of Edgar's intestines, Luna struggled to remain standing and watched Edgar weaken with each passing breath. A malicious glint shone in Edgar's gaze as he stared at the stream of blood pouring from the wound he had inflicted to her abdomen. "I got you, you flea-ridden bitch. Say hello to your master in hell."

The last thing Edgar saw before death claimed him was Luna stumbling out the front door.

Chapter 8

CLAUDIA WATCHED her grandson's health deteriorate before her eyes. It had been hours since the last, and most severe wound appeared on Leroy's body, a deep puncture to his abdomen. Blood seeped through the bed sheets and his breathing became shallower with every passing minute. As the sun began to rise, she knew her beloved grandbaby was minutes away from breathing his last breath. She closed her eyes and prayed his transition to whatever lay beyond this earthly realm was a peaceful one.

A faint scratching sounded at the front door.

Reluctant to leave Leroy's side for even a second, she sped to the door and sobbed in surprise to see Luna, looking as haggard and beaten as Leroy. "My precious babies." Claudia cried, dropping to her knees and squeezing Luna tightly, despite the gore and grime covering her body, then brought her to Leroy and helped her onto the bed.

Luna shuffled to the head of the bed and softly licked Leroy's face, which was hot to the touch. His forehead was covered with perspiration and his breaths were coming in short gasps. Luna brought her head down until she was nose to nose with Leroy, and her eyes began to glow with the same amber illumination as before.

Leroy's eyes fluttered weakly and Claudia caught a glimpse of the same glow through the cracks of his eyelids. The circular bite mark on his face began to fade away. In seconds, his face was smooth and unblemished. She watched in amazement as the inflamed tissue around Leroy's broken nose started to heal. The bruises faded from deep purple, to brown, and then his normal complexion within moments. Her sobs of heartache turned into delighted gasps as Leroy's eyes fluttered open and he drew a deep breath.

Leroy suddenly sprang to a seated position in the bed and wrapped his arms around Luna as she slumped over, barely breathing. "Luna, why?" he uttered in anguish, clutching his treasured tonal tightly against his chest.

Claudia, crying tears of joy, draped an arm around Leroy's shoulder in a comforting embrace. Confusion clouded her eyes as she asked, "What just happened?"

"Luna. She... she... gave her last bit of energy so I could survive." Leroy wept, understanding the depth of love his tonal had for him. He knew his life would never be the same again.

Claudia held her grandson in silence until he was composed enough to tear himself away from Luna.

With his grandmother's assistance, Leroy climbed out of bed and respectfully wrapped Luna's body in preparation for her burial.

Once completed, Claudia suggested he take a shower. As he was doing so, she busied herself changing the bedclothes and making breakfast. He was weak, famished, and in desperate need of solid food after weeks of only consuming liquids.

An hour later, Leroy and Claudia were seated at the breakfast table when they heard a gentle knock on the front door. Leroy's glum demeanor was replaced with joy when Jae walked in. He jumped up from his seat and rushed over to the entryway and wrapped Jae in a tight embrace.

"Leroy!" Jae gasped in delight. "How... When did you...?"

Leroy stepped back, separating himself from his partner to get a better view of him. He smiled broadly and then, without a word, knelt down on one knee.

"What are you doing?" Jae asked, confused.

Leroy reached into his pocket and withdrew the ring Claudia had been holding for him since the incident. Its glassy surface reflected brightly in the morning sunlight. "Jae, you are, without a doubt, the greatest gift I could have ever asked for. Our love is the kind you never really have to think about. We don't have to try too hard or convince ourselves of the reasons we love each other. It's simply there. It's the most important part of everything I do, and I want to spend the rest of my life with you. Will you marry me?"

Jae's face was wet with tears. He answered without hesitation. "Yes! Absolutely, I'll marry you."

Leroy carefully slipped the ring onto Jae's finger and stood up to embrace his soon-to-be husband.

Claudia watched the scene unfold from a distance and let out a gasp of delight. She hurried towards both men with arms open wide and hugged them tightly.

Moments later, the trio separated, each one wiping away tears. Then, Jae said, "Hang on a second. I almost forgot something." He turned and left the house, returning seconds later with his hands behind his back.

"What is it?" Leroy asked. "What are you hiding?"

Jae stretched out his arms, to reveal a small, black puppy. "I found it just outside your door as I was walking up. I think it's a stray. I figured we could foster it together," he said, smiling at Leroy, handing him the pup.

The dog playfully licked Leroy's nose as he cradled it in his arms. He wasn't sure if it was the light playing tricks on him, but

Leroy swore he saw the puppy's eyes flash with an exquisite amber shimmer.

Claudia also noticed, and gasped in wonder as she saw the same glint mirrored in Leroy's eyes.

She looked from the puppy to Leroy who stared back at her, tears glimmering in his eyes. "Luna?" Claudia whispered.

Leroy smiled and nodded his head affirmatively.

Rowland Bercy, Jr. burst onto the writing scene five years ago and has quickly established himself as a talented storyteller. His novella Unbortion was met with both acclaim and controversy, earning him top honors at the 2020 American Fiction Awards and a finalist spot in the 2019 International Book Awards. Readers who seek to push their own boundaries while delving into the darker aspects of life will find his work exciting and rewarding.

Rowland's writing experience has been a rollercoaster ride of excitement and uncertainty, taking him on an adventure unlike any other. Throughout his journey, he encountered numerous talented authors and many devoted fans who have motivated and supported him every step of the way.

He can be found on social media platforms like Facebook, Instagram, and Tik Tok, as well as on his website: www.rowland-bercyjr.com

BLOOD AND SPRITE

JUDITH SONNET

Blood was such a good boy, and when he fell sick, it had just about ripped Laramie's heart to tatters. He couldn't stand to watch his once energetic and lively dog now lie on a mat and shit uncontrollably. And when Blood sniffed at the gray gel that sputtered out of his loosened rectum, he looked frightened of it. As if it was acidic, and it was eating its way out of him.

Stupidly, Laramie had hoped that Belinda Matthews could cure the old pooch. He figured his soul was worth forfeiting so long as his dog was yipping and yapping just as he used to.

He knocked on Belinda's door, and when she answered she was nude. He'd been shocked, because although her face was as wrinkled as a rotten apple, she did have a good set of knockers on her.

"What is it? Whaddya want?" Belinda snapped. She smelled like smoke and incense, and he saw white powder on her hands. Apparently, he'd interrupted one of her rites.

Laramie took his hat off and held it to his chest. He bowed his head reverently, casting his eyes away from the hag's form.

While it rained and thundered behind him, he stood at Belinda's doorway and explained his situation to her. She listened intently, her hand holding the edge of the door as if she was ready to slam it at any given moment.

After telling her about Blood, Laramie waited patiently.

"I ain't in the business of resurrection. I'm a witch, not a necromancer," Belinda seethed, as if he'd insulted her.

"I'm right awful sowrry, ma'am. But I don't know the difference."

"Necromancers deal with Death Magick," Belinda said.

"Well, do you recommend one fer me ta seek out then, if you ain't up fer the job?"

Belinda scowled, then chuckled. "You ain't too bright, is ya?"

"Nah, ma'am. I done flunked outta school in the third grade. Well, my pappy took me outta it. Said I was old 'nough ta start workin'. Reckon he was right. I wasn't taken ta readin' an' writin' anyhow."

Belinda dithered. "Well, if yer dog ain't dead yet, then maybe I can get some healin' spirits ta pay attention to him. But listen up, Mr. Laramie Capulet . . . you ain't never been to one of my rites before, and you'll probably never wanna come back to 'nother afterwards. You'll be wantin' to run, or argue, or fight back. You'll be so scared I'm willin' to wager you'll piss them britches you got on. But, Laramie, if you run . . . you'll have more than a dead dog on yer hands. You'll have vexing spirits, who won't leave you alone 'til the day you put a gun in yer mouth and blow that useless appendage between yer shoulders clear off. You hear me?"

"Yes'um. I hear ya. I'll stick through it, even though I'm a mite terrified already."

"Come on in. An' be sure to wipe them boots of a'fore ya do."

Laramie stepped into Belinda's home. It was warm and bright inside, which was surprising considering the peeled paint and gnarled trees growing in the front. The house looked, from the outside, like a haunted place. Inside, it was just a regular house. Except, of course, for the naked witch that was now hobbling toward the living room.

Laramie followed close by, keeping his eyes off her rumpled butt—which looked like a closed fist—and the blue-black veins in her legs.

"You threw eggs at my house, din'cha?"

"Huh?" Laramie asked.

"Issa'ight. All you kids do. Bitch to clean up, especially in the hotter days, when folks toss eggs and then they get cooked 'fore I can wipe 'em up. I think you threw yours 'round Halloween, though. Very rude night to bother me. Ya ought know how important that night is ta witches."

"I'm sorry," Laramie said. "I was awful young and real dumb. I admit it. I went along with some friends, and we threw them eggs right on your doorstep. Thought it was a good laugh too."

"Well, glad ta hear you admit it. Some folks him-haw and cast blame when they get called out."

"Nope, not me," Laramie said with some pride. "I did it. And I'm sorry. And I'm sorry I didn't apologize sooner. Should've come by and said so if I was actually the Good Christian I claim to be."

Belinda snorted. "There won't be much of that Christian left in ya after this."

That scared him, but he chose not to reflect on it. Laramie walked behind Belinda and joined her in the living room. There were no sofas or sitting places, no ornamentation, and no carpeting. There was a circle of slat in the rooms center, and a few waxy piles that were topped with flickering wicks. In the dim light, the shadows seemed to crawl like earthworms.

"Yer gonna wanter get nekkid."

"N-naked?" Laramie asked.

"And that'll be the least of it, boy. You want yer dog to get better?"

"Yes'um," Laramie gulped. "But I mean ... n-n-naked?"

Belinda rolled her eyes. "You've seen mine. Don't you think it right an' proper I see yers?"

That didn't help, but he thought of Blood. The old dog was wheezing instead of barking.

Slowly, Laramie peeled his duds off and left them piled in the corner. He cupped his penis in his hands, and it felt hot against his palms. Like his little pardner was running a fever. Although, "little pardner" was an ironic nickname. Laramie's penis was log-like, and its head was a bald thumb.

Blushing, he stepped into the salt circle and waited for instructions.

"We're gonna be summoning a spirit of healing. His name is Grathus-Issliom-Olfeck. He's very particular about that name, so I want you to practice it a bit like it's yer ABC's."

She coached him on the name until he'd gotten it down.

"I-is he a demon?" Laramie asked.

"Havin' second doubts about yer fondness fer ol' Blood?"

"N-no. I just figure I oughta know."

Without answering, Belinda went over to one of the darker corners. She vanished briefly from sight, and when she returned he was startled to see a gleaming letter opener in her left fist.

She sliced her right thumb like a split grape and ran the blood along her brow. Then, she squatted and began to inscribe symbols of the floor. She winced when a kernel of salt touched her wound, but the pain didn't stop her.

After she'd drawn a row of stars and two upturned crosses—which really scared Laramie, but he held his tongue—she began to doodle new symbols. Symbols he'd never seen before in all his life. Some looked like wicked smiles, while others reminded him of fractured spiderwebs. They were surprisingly thin and detailed, considering she was drawing with dripping blood.

After she'd finished, she held the letter opener toward him. "Take it."

Her sweat had made its handle wet, and he noticed multiple rusty stains along its edges.

Does she gotta cut herself every time she performs these rites?

"Wh-what do you want me ta do?" Laramie asked.

"Cut yourself."

Laramie swallowed.

"On yer piss-hole."

Laramie's heart stopped in his chest.

"What?" he asked, outraged and wounded all at once.

"It ain't gotta be that deep. Yer gonna wanna make it look like a little crucifix. The slit being the body of the cross, and the cut being its arms," Belinda explained. "Just a little nick. You'd get worse from shaving."

"I don't know if I—"

"You said you wouldn't step outta this. Well, here's yer test. Either you cut yer pecker, or your dog dies, and you wind up haunted. We've already caught Grathus-Issliom-Olfeck's attention," she indicated the patterns she'd etched in her own blood. "And you don't wanna disappoint him, Laramie. Believe you me."

Laramie gripped his penis and turned it up so he could look at the hole. It seemed to gasp in his grip, like a fish brought up from the water.

He considered laying the edge of the letter opener against the hole and quickly drawing it back. He imagined blood welling up from the miniscule injury and running down his urethra and along the ridges of his shaft.

It really wouldn't be that bad.

Just like a bee sting.

Not that bad.

Not that bad.

But it was. When he cut the head of his cock, he about fainted. He recalled, with terror, the time he'd found a leech on the underside of his scrotum after swimming at the local watering hole. That was easy-street compared to this.

"Oh, Christ!"

"Now *massurbate!*" Belinda commanded.

"What?"

"Quick! 'Fore ya stop bleeding! Quick!"

"I'm feelin' . . . I need a doctor!" Laramie stumbled on his feet. He felt as if he was about to pass out. His vision blurred and his mouth was dry. "Oh, Lord. Oh, Lord. My jimmy—"

He almost bolted when Belinda crossed the circle and gripped his cock in one of her skinny hands. It felt like he was being jerked off by a skeleton, but he allowed it to happen. He rocked his hips, hoping to aide in the woman's dismal handplay.

The head of his rod was burning, and he'd dropped the letter opener. It sat near his feet, gleaming with fresh redness.

Laramie closed his eyes and tried to picture something else. Something that was actually good and sexy.

He saw his ex-girlfriend from high school. She'd been a ripe plum of a woman, with brown hair, big titties, and a butt that got all oily and damp when he fucked it.

He imagined making love to her in the barn.

She'd hitched her skirts up around her hips and pulled her panties down to her ankles, and when she bent over her vagina smiled at him like a friend.

"You wanna put it in or are ya jus' gonna look at it?" she'd asked impatiently after a few seconds had passed.

Yes. That'd been a real good fuck. I about blew my brains outta my peter after putting it to her in that barn. And she'd cum too.

...I think ...

Laramie enjoyed the memory of her softness and sweetness, and he kept his eyes closed so the illusion wasn't shattered. He knew one look at the woman that was actually massaging his manhood would kill the healthy boner he'd developed.

He thought of another girl. This was one he knew from the local bar he attended on Friday nights—and sometimes Saturday mornings, when none of the staff had the energy to move him out to the street.

This woman worked behind the bar. She always wore black tank tops, and rarely kept a bra on her bouncing breasts. Her skin was leathery, and her hair was a luscious black, and he could watch her sway from patron to patron all night. He was also fascinated by her naked armpits, because they looked like cups of flesh. So smooth and deep, he could just loose a whole hand up 'em—

He imagined her crawling over the bar toward him, her butt high in the air behind her like a squirrels tail. He imagined her gripping him by the hair and forcing his face into her sweaty left armpit. He breathed in her musky odor as she rubbed his face like a loofa.

"You like that, boy? You like the way I stink after a hard day's work?" she asked, both cruel and playful.

And yes, Laramie did. He liked it so much, the very idea of it made him spurt.

He shook as his erection jumped in Belinda's hand. Brought back to the present, he felt his cheeks redden and his asshole tighten as his semen leapt into Belinda's cupped palm. She collected as much of his ropey expulsion as she could.

His cum was stained rusty red with blood.

"Thar we go!" Belinda moaned, happy with the result of her labor.

"I'm awful sorry, ma'am. I dunno what came over me—"

"Shuddup," Belinda said as she landed on her rump, and then began to lick the blood and cum from her hand.

Laramie watched with growing horror as she ate up his offering. Just thinking about how rancid those combined liquids must taste—he about lost his lunch right then and there. But he squeezed his throat closed and kept his eyes open.

Before long, Belinda had lapped everything up, save for a chunky, curdled patch of white foam that rested between her index and ring finger. Her pruned tongue snaked out and gathered even that sticky particle, and then her hand was sheened in nothing but saliva.

"Wh-why'd you do such a nasty thing like that?" Laramie asked.

Belinda laid on her back and spread her legs. Her shriveled cunt revolted him.

"Follow my lead," she said. "Stand between my legs, and chant with me."

Warily, he did as she wanted. He started to wonder if there was no Magick. Maybe all of this was a ruse to get a young man to play a perverted game with her. Maybe she was getting off on this.

"Grathus-Issliom-Olfeck. Lord of healing. Lord of minded

organs and untangled veins. Lord of being and of betterment. Hear us."

Laramie stumbled through the declaration. He was thankful to get the name of the invocation's subject correct, but the rest was butchered by anxiety.

"Ram-N*ää*. Iä! Iä! In our court, we invite you, Grathus-Issliom-Olfeck! Lord! We worship you! We worship you!"

Laramie felt a heaviness in his bowels. It was sudden and burbling. He clenched his sphincter and reached behind him to hold his buns together. The last thing he wanted to do was take a nervous shit in the middle of Belinda's living room.

"Ma'am . . . " he whined.

"Ram-N*ää*. Iä! Iä!"

"Ma'am! I'm sorry, but I've gotta go!"

"We call upon you—"

"It's an emergency!" his bowels seemed to deflate as the feces was carted through them. His stomach burned and his anus yawned, despite his wishes. "Please!"

A deluge fell between his cheeks and splattered against the floor. Embarrassed and humiliated, Laramie tried his best to *catch* his diarrhea shower, even as it slipped out of him and sheeted his thighs.

Oh, Christ!

She's gonna kick me outta this house, and then she'll tell folks in town. I'll never hear the end of it.

Laramie done crapped himself at weird ol' Belinda Matthews house! He looked like a pigpen when he done waddled outta that house!

It was bad! Real bad! A right mudslide!

And the smell!

The odor of his filth was like a stagnant pond on a hot summer day. A pond filled with bloated, dead fish, which were floating on the surface, their bellies expanding and bursting under the nuclear power of the sun.

Laramie began to cry as he fell into a desperate squat. It felt like he was pushing writhing worms out of his gut. The feces burned the rim of his anus, like hot sauce on soft lips.

He suddenly knew *exactly* how Blood felt. Crapping and being ashamed of it. He wondered if he should've just put the old pooch out of his misery.

He looked at the growing mud puddle beneath him. It was trickling across the floor, running toward—

"Belinda! Look out!" Laramie shouted.

But it was too late. His sickness was coagulating around her rear. It impossibly seemed to crawl up her flesh and circle into her cunt, like scum down a hairy drain.

Oh, Lord! If this ain't the weirdest day of my damn fool life!

He hoped Belinda would notice that his sentient waste was being vacuumed up by her gaping cunt, but she seemed unbothered by it. Even as her belly began to swell and grow below her ribcage. She continued chanting. Laramie followed suit, stepping back into the chant. He was worried he'd displease her if he tore his focus away from the ritual.

Then, Belinda stopped. She lay still.

Laramie wondered if she was dead.

Her belly deflated, and something red tumbled from the gash between her legs. It was the size of a rabbit, and its skin was flecked with many fluids. Vaginal juice, enzymes... semen, blood, and feces.

The little creature squalled the second it hit the floor. Its limbs kicked and its head thrashed.

"Oh, Jesus!" Laramie cried.

Belinda sat up and scooped the creature into her arms. She fit one of her massive breasts into its mouth, and its screams were replaced with deep suction noises. Even though she was an elderly woman, her full breasts fed the demon without hesitation.

"Wh-what is it?"

"A gift from Grathus-Issliom-Olfeck. It's a Healing Sprite. You'll have to butcher it yourself, and then feed it to your dog."

"*What?*" Laramie's jaw fell open. The shit was beginning to grow sticky on the backs of his legs, and in the damp crevice of his buttocks. He wanted to scrub his skin raw, and he wanted to forget all about this crazy night he had shared with Belinda.

"You'll clean it the same you do any wild animal. But collect the blood in a bucket. If the meat don't take and yer pooch ain't healed ... then let him drink the blood. It might do the trick. If the dog does feel better, then you can drink the blood yerself next time you ain't feelin' up to snuff. I promise, it don't go bad. Sprite blood never does."

Laramie got dressed in stunned silence. When he was ready to leave, Belinda deposited the squirming atrocity in his arms. It looked like a human baby, were it not for its long, rat-like snout and the spade-shaped hands. And it had a pigtail like growth coming from its belly, but no genitals between its kicking legs.

"Y-you serious? I'm supposed ta feed this to my ol' Blood?"

"Yes, I am. If you want Blood to bark for another season, you give it to 'im even if'n he don't wan' it."

Laramie nodded. "Okay. Wh-what can I pay ya? Fer yer services?"

Belinda patted his back and said, "You just promise me something, and we'll call it square."

"Yes?"

"When you say yer prayers at night ... you don't send 'em ta God. Ya hear?"

"Wha—how—how come?"

Belinda looked very serious. Even more so than she'd been during the perverse ritual.

"Because he won't have 'em now that you done this."

"I'm a bit confused, ma'am. But … sure."

"That's a good boy." She led him to the front door and opened it. As he stepped into the rain, she shouted behind him, "And don't go throwin' eggs at houses no more, son! Yer lucky I decided not to hex you the way I did Tyson Barley and Bucky Davis."

He thought of his teenaged chums. Tyson had died on the toilet, and Bucky had died with his face in a bowl of breakfast cereal and milk. Both deaths had occurred not five days after Halloween. He'd been too brain-dumb to think there'd been a correlation.

Laramie swallowed hard, then raced away from Belinda's house and to his car …

He hadn't fed the Sprite to Blood. He'd been too afraid to.

Instead, he'd taken the creature and threw it over a bridge and into a running creek, which silenced its continuous cries. He'd felt guilty about it for weeks, but he also knew that putting Blood down was the right and proper thing to do. Even after all the pain, humiliation, and fright he'd suffered, he just didn't think it a good idea to chop up the demonic creature and potentially taint the hound dog's soul with its meat.

He'd given Blood a bone to chew, and although his munching was weak, it seemed to cheer the old dog up. Then, Laramie had taken his best pal behind the barn and shot him in the head. That about crushed his heart to smithereens.

Although it hurt, Laramie found he was resting easy. Because he knew that Blood was at peace, and that if there was such a thing as Doggy Heaven then Blood was certainly chasing rabbits and squirrels to his heart's content up in them clouds.

Maybe he even had a set of angel wings and a halo over his rumpled head.

That made Laramie smile, even when he'd felt like sobbing.

Judith Sonnet is a very sad girl. She writes gross and disturbing horror books, and she collects old paperbacks as well as 70's action movies. She grew up in Missouri, but now she lives in Utah. She's trans, asexual, and is an abuse and suicide survivor. If you want to know more about her, check her out on Facebook . . . or contact her through your nearest Ouija board.

WE HUNT AT NIGHT

DUNCAN RALSTON

We hunt at night. They's slower in the dark, prob'ly harder fer em to see, an' Rosco can sniff em out just as good as in the daytime. All I hafta do is keep a close eye awn him so's I can pick em off when he starts goin nuts.

The missus don't love us goin out after dark, but it's better'n waitin around fer em to close in awn the farm wall her an' the li'lun are sleepin. Folks'd prob'ly say we was dumb as dog shit bringin a baby into this world, bein the way it is now, but we'd been tryin fer years an' wouldn't you know it? Just 'bout a week into the end of the dang world, turns out Jody May's got a bun in the oven.

They say when God closes a door, He opens a winduh. Well, He sure as hell closed one big fuckuva door this time, an' I'ma do my best to protect the li'l winduh He provided. Life has to go on, even under the worst circumstances. Anyone in one of those shithole countries'd tell you that, which I guess even the good ol' U.S. of A. is now, come to thank. An' these are just about the worst circumstances I can imagine.

This all started with a virus, an' not like the one that kilt some folks an' put the economy in the shitter when they stuck us in cornteen. This one hit hard an' it hit fast. Wasn't no wait a couple days an' stick a Q-Tip up your booger-maker to figger out if it's a flu or not. Someone got bit, they got sick in about a hour or less, 'pendin awn they metabolism an' size. Only it ain't just coughin an' wheezin an' layin up in a hospital bed if you happen to got insurance, it's a full-blown rabid, chompin-on-the-neighbors kinda sick. The kinda sick that ends with a bullet to the head 'stead of a needle an' a lollypop.

Speakin of rabid, Rosco's just bout the only dog I seen ain't got the bug. Shot a whole lotta dogs since the world went to shit —cats, too. He been lucky, I guess. I don't figger he's immune or nothin. Don't figger anybody's immune from this one, we ain't that lucky. These are the End Times they talk about in the Bible, sure nuff. Just ain't got bit yet, that's how come. Rosco's a wily sucker. Smarter'n any dog I had before'm, even when I was a boy an' we had that Lassie dog named Curtis. That mutt was smart as a whip, but he still woulda been zombie fricasee, 'cause he weren't wily like Rosco.

I ain't sayin Rosco's the perfect dog. Oft times he come home reekin to high heaven 'cause of rollin in some animal's shit or another. Jody May had to warsh im in tomato juice more'n once. An' heck, if he gets hode of some ode bone out ere in the woods, I pert much hafta pry his goddamn jaws open with both hands to get that sucker to let go. But all that's part of what makes im such a good hunter. He's a purebred Mountain Cur, smallest one from a litter of eight. Smart nuff to know not to bite them thangs out ere, since he can tell if someone got bit just by smellin em an' knows they ain't right. That's how he spared us gettin bit when Tom Genessee come over 'cross the tobacco field. Rosco jump up from his spot by the farplace where it's warm an' got to sniffin the air even before Tom climbed the fence. Time Tom got near the house, Rosco was awready bayin at the door like he does when he got a scent awn one of em thangs an' Tom was all, *I ain't bit, I ain't bit*, with his hands in the air. But he had blood awn his hands an' Rosco's nose don't lie, so I shot Tom dead awn the porch. Turns out the sumbitch got bit, all right. Whole damn family got bit. Had to go 'round their place'n pick em off, an' the ones that bit em, just to make sure they wasn't gon' come 'round the house awn instinct like Tom done.

He's real good with the baby, too—Rosco, not Tom. Don't get aggressive or nothin, an' protective as all hell. Heck, I bet if it came down to Baby Mellie or me, that damn dog'd pick the girl, an' I cain't say I blame im.

Perfect li'l angel, that one.

Jody May wanted to name er Melanie after er maw, who got sick that first week when most of the deaths was in the ode folks homes an' hospitals an' such. That was a couple days before the cornteen an' about a week before the whole world went to shit. She loved er maw an' I guess I did, too. Mel was a strong, proud woman who raised four kids awn er own after her husban' died over in Iraq back when Bush Senior called the shots. I knew Russell, he was a no-good drunk an' hard awn his kids, 'specially Mel an' the girls. No big loss, is what I mean. Mel was better off without 'im, even if she had to stretch ever last dollar to the limit.

So namin Mellie after the weeun's mamaw was a kinda tribute, an' also she hoped Mellie'd grow up strong like er own maw taught Jody May to. World like the one she'll be livin in once me an' Jody May's gone, she gon' hafta be strong or she ain't gon' make it far, an' that's the God's honest truth.

ME AN' Rosco gotta make a run fer supplies tonight. Like I said, Jody May don't like fer us to go out at night an' leave er alone with the baby, an' tell the truth I don't like to do it. But if me an' Rosco *don't* go out an' pick off as many of em as we can, more chance we get slaughtered like the O'Malleys an' the Genessees an' the Thompsons an' all of em other folk within twenny miles of town. I done a few supply drives with Rosco the past few months an' they ain't a soul out ere who ain't sick, least not anyone who wanna be found. An' I get that, not wantin to be found, considerin how rough things got with em army fellas an' whatnot runnin through town with machine guns after the cornteen just to make things even shittier fer the rest of us. That is, 'fore all of em got sick an' died themself, then come back again with their faces an' limbs rottin off, prob'ly their peckers too. Least they forgot how to shoot. Small favors an' awl that.

I let Rosco sit up front with me in the truck when we head out. Some fellas don't like their hounds to ride with em, rather have em in the back, but I figger, better to have 'im close if things get rough, like they sometimes do. Though after I put Tom an' Tammy an' their kids outta their misery, ere's been less of em out ere to shoot. Figger ere gon' come a day when we can kick back an' not hafta thank 'bout em things bein out ere anymore. Praytor wasn't ever a big town to start with, maybe a hunnert awn a good day, hunnert fifty tops during the fair, an' we only got a handfulla farms awn th'outskirts. Nothin else around fer miles, an' the closest city's a hunnert miles southeast. Maybe em city critters'll come wanderin out this way someday, but winters are harsh an' em hills make fer tough climbin. Wouldn't be surprised if me an' Rosco wasn't able to kick up our boots so to speak come next summer. Fall at the latest.

I drive slow, purrin along like a tomcat awn the prowl. Lights off. Gotta wait fer the eyes to adjust to the dark first, but once they do it's pert much drivin awn instinct, like how Rosco hunts awn instinct. I know the roads so good I could prob'ly drive em with my eyes closed, but then you never know what might pop up outta nowhere, like a hoard or a deer. Deer didn't get sick, thank the Lord, we got nuff venzun to feed a army, even though em army fellas'd prob'ly rather eat me an' the wife, that is if ere's any left of 'em. *Something* could run out into the road anyways, an' me an' Rosco'd be dead in a ditch an' the missus an' littlun'd prob'ly starve to death without us.

Gotta get some lag bolts to fix the fence—Tom climbin over it so easy got me thankin I should fortify the farm a li'l better, prob'ly shoulda done that when em tweaker porch thiefs come 'round the house 'fore all this shit went down, askin to use the phone like I was born yesterday. Gotta get some extra wire to keep em sick dogs an' coyotes outta the chicken coop, too. To be honest, with all the deer walkin 'round out ere em chickens're kinda moot, but Jody May says variety is the spice of life, plus she likes them eggs fer cookin. So we head to the hardware store in Praytor hopin they got some long screws, otherwise we gotta drive all the way to the city an' the roads are jammed up the closer you get like an ode timer's bunghole 'fore his mornin cup o' prune juice. Not to mention all em dead critters walkin around jes lookin for some fresh meat like me to chow down on.

Funny thing about Praytor. Back when we was kids, we used to say "Praytor God we make it outta this shithole alive." But even though ere was fuck all to do when we was young, most of us stayed here after we was done with school just like our folks did. An' maybe the ones that stayed didn't make it out alive, but neither did anyone that left town either, I bet.

Once we get to town the drive goes slower, 'cause of the trucks an' Tucker Beck's rolled-over tractor an' whatnot in the middle of the road. Gotta weave around em until Main Street, then park by the town square an' walk the rest of the way 'cause of the barricades the army fellas put up fer reasons unknown to anyone but the dumbest of fucks. Just how a barricade was gonna prevent dead folks walkin 'round it is anyone's guess. I s'pose maybe they was tryna stop people from lootin or somethin but they all dead now an' so's all the folks who run them stores, so the joke's awn em, ain't it?

I close the truck door real quiet an' Rosco jumps out an' scurries awn ahead, sniffin along the asphalt. First thing he does it piss awn the barricade, an' if I hadn't pissed out by the shed myself 'fore we left the house I'd do the same. Fuckin good fer nuthin army idiots. Was a pleasure to put em assholes down once I got the chance, that's fer damn sure. Got some fine weaponry outta em fellas, too, but I always prefer to hunt with my trusty ode ought-six.

Rosco trots awn ahead a ways past the hardware store—ain't his fault, he don't know the names of places, but I could let im run off now an' he'd find his way back home lickety-split. I call im over an' he hurries awn back like a good boy. Big store window's already smashed in from the last time we needed somethin here, so it's real easy to walk awn in. We'll get what we need if they have em an' be in an' out in a jiff.

Rosco follows me past the checkout an' over to the building materials aisle. Used to be this store was just hardware an' power tools an' random fixtures, but they started gettin cute around Y2K an' brought in all kinds of crap ain't got no business bein in a hardware store. Ere's a rack of Halloween costumes an' shelves of fancy candles an' all manner of Bed Bath & Beyond shit 'fore we can even get to the fasteners. If society didn't get flushed down the big ol' proverbial shitter, I figger eventually it woulda got to the point where they'd turn the ropes an' chains aisle into some BDSM paradise an' call it a job well done. Maybe put a sign under where they keep the sparkplugs tellin folks you can also shove em up yer ass.

Prob'ly fer the best God decided to call in His debts.

Gotta turn awn the headlamp fer this part. Tellin screws an' bolts apart's hard nuff in the daylight. 5/64s an' 1/8s an' 3/16s an' wood screws an' metal screws an' screw this shit, I cain't find the sunsabitches even with the lamp. I'm just 'bout to give up awn the whole damn enterprise an' call Rosco back to the truck when one of the Halloween costumes lunges out of the rack an' grabs hode of my fuckin arm.

It's dressed up like that fuckin Eye-talian plumber, the green one not the red one, an' I guess it musta been hidin in the round-about rack 'cause I didn't see it comin in an' Rosco musta run awn ahead to the dog chow he found last time we was here. It's got me pushed up against the li'l bins of fasteners—my mind's awn survival otherwise I'da made a joke 'bout bein screwed or somethin—an' it's got ahode of my goddamn arm so's I cain't get to my rifle, slung over th'other one. I'm hodin the smelly critter back, an' it's chompin away like it's tryna eat the air between us. Its breath smells like the used tampon basket in a gas station toilet, an' that fake mustache is hangin onto his rotten upper lip by a red cunt hair.

The fact that I'm 'bout to get ate by a grown-ass man in a goddamn Halloween costume don't elude me, an' I guess I gotta find the humor in it or die mad. I'm not dead yet though, still got my forearm hodin the critter back by the throat, but this one seems to've got that tweaker strength an' I cain't get my other arm free to grab the rifle, pinned up as it is against a li'l bin of screws.

Just when the fucker's 'bout to bite my goddamn nose off— be a mercy, considerin how bad its breath reeks—Rosco comes skitterin around the corner, barkin up a storm, runnin tords us.

That dumb sumbitch critter turns its head awn instinct, still chewin the air, an' that gives me a second to grab a handful of whatever fasteners happen to be in the bin an' fling em at the fucker's stupid face. It lets go of my arm—I see one of em long screws I was lookin for's stuck in its right eye, makin clear goo ooze out like an uncooked egg white—an' I make a grab fer the thirty-ought-six, swinging it up under the fucker's jaw an' firin a single shot through his dome lightnin quick.

Lights out. Yuns don't got to go home, you just cain't stay here.

Mario or th'other fella crumples like a sack of shit an' Rosco scurries over to me, climin all over me an' lickin my face as I slide to the floor in sheer exhaustion. "Good boy, good boy," I tell im, 'cause even if he didn't smell the fucker in his hellbent race to the chow aisle, he did save my goddamn life, well more'n once now, an' I figger he deserves a treat or two fer that.

Plus, we found em screws, so it's a win-win.

LATER THAT SAME NIGHT, Rosco sits in his spot by the far, chompin awn a leg bone from the buck we got th'other day, wall me an' Jody May eat venzun stew an' Mellie's got that puréed vegetable shit er maw cooked up fer er from er garden patch, even though most of it ends up awn Mellie's face or the floor. Rosco'd normally be under ere lappin it up an' waitin fer more if he didn't have no bone to gnaw on.

"We gon' hafta take that away from im 'fore it starts to splinter," Jody May says, eyin him real cautious.

"Yup," I tell er. "Jes gon' let im get the meat off the dang thang first. Least I could give im fer savin my ass."

"Watch yer tongue in front of the baby, Bent," she goes, an' slurps up another spoonful. She makes a mean stew, I gotta say. Makes a mean just about anythin, considerin the times an' all. "How many times that dog save your life now?"

"More'n I can count. He's a good boy. Ain't ye, Rosco?"

Rosco gives me hound dog eyes over the bone like I'm 'bout to snatch it away. An' Jody May's right, we lost Curtis 'cause he done swallowed a gut fulla bone splinters, chewed is insides all up. No way I'm 'bout to lose Rosco like that, too. Specially since he's prob'ly the last dog we'll ever own, 'less he finds a lady mutt out ere that ain't sick an' we have ourselves a litter. It's a big responsibility, repopulatin the world an' all that, but if any dog could do it, it'd be Rosco. Sumbitch got more illegitimate kids'n a sailor awn shore leave. Hell, pretty sure I already had to put a couple of em down myself, em bein sick an' all. Rosco didn't seem to mind, if they was.

After supper, I get a far goin in the hearth wall Jody May washes up. Rosco's got all the meat off the bone so I trick him with a ball, an' after he goes runnin fer it he only notices I tricked im after he's got the ball in his mouth an' he drops it with a look like he cain't believe he got suckered again. I put the bone awn the mantle so he cain't reach it an' he comes back over an' plops down in his usual spot with a moan.

I pull up a chair 'side Mellie at the table an' shake a rattle for er. She goggles an' I get a smile, with a li'l bit more drool than I was 'spectin. Jody May's left a li'l rag she used to wipe up the girl's mess awn the table, so I use it to wipe up the spit an' get up an' toss the rag in the sink.

"Need some help?"

Jody May's dryin off the last few pots an' tableware. "I'm good. Why'n't sit an' read by the far?"

"Okay then."

Not much to read these days 'side from a dwindlin stack of

ode newspapers I kept fer kindlin an' a few mystery books I saw fit to scrounge from the pharmacy, but sometimes it's comfortin to remember how good we had it 'fore the Great Flush. We had our share of problems, sure. Poor folk gettin poorer wall the rich took far more'n their share, too many folks hopped up awn hillbilly heroin an' meth, folks killin each other fer a difference in opinion or the way they look or 'cause they got the wrong colors on. But common folk could still come together'n break bread now'n then, or at least be civil when we had to interact with people we might not get along with, an' not bite each other's goddamn heads off. Unlike these days, where the expression's more'n just a metaphor.

I read about the wars overseas an' 'member people just 'bout wantin to kill each other over shit that had nothin to do with em. Why'd we get so mad 'bout that, mad nuff to disown our own families an' kill our neighbors? Sometimes I thank we're better off now, nobody to worry 'bout but me an' Jody May an' the girl. But then what's the point of all this if Mellie won't have nobody of er own to grow ode with? Sometimes I figger we'd all be best off if I shot the two of em an' Rosco an' put the barrel in my own mouth an' just shut out the lights awn the whole damn business. Closin time at the human tavern.

Thoughts like that never fail to make me choke up a bit, an' I ain't cried since we put down Curtis when I was ten. Ain't no way I could bring myself to do that to Jody May an' Mellie, or even Rosco an' my own self. I know Billy Chambers who used to run the hardware store done it, kilt is wife'n two boys an' hung imself in the barn. Left a helluva mess to waltz in on, 'specially since I just come round to ask if they had a jump fer my truck. Found Billy first, then th'others. Sumbitch musta kilt the boys wall they was sleepin. Woulda looked just like li'l angels if em halos wasn't like Chef Boyardee with disco rice festerin in em bits of brain an' skull an' awl.

Jody May hangs the towel awn the rack an' puts Mellie in er crib in the bedroom, then comes over an' rubs my shoulders. It feels nice. I was never the type for massages 'fore Jody May, but she does magic with em fingers of ers. Gets kinks an' sore spots I didn't even know I had 'til she's workin er knuckles in em.

After the far dies down, I put it the rest of the way out an' we head fer bed.

Jody May gets awn er knees 'side the bed an' prays, like she does ever night. I don't find much reason to pray these days. Wasn't much of a religious man 'fore the Great Flush, an' havin to put a bullet in just 'bout ever'one I know hasn't given me much reason to pledge my faith to a higher power now, even with Miracle Mellie sleepin soundly in the crib at the foot of the bed.

Jody May finishes up er prayer with a whispered "Amen," an' climbs under the covers to snuggle up next to me as I blow out the light.

Already the nights are getting chilly. Gon' be winter soon an' then who knows how in the hell we gon' make it.

"BLOW OUT THE LIGHTS," I tell Jody May.

It's prob'ly two weeks from the night I was thankin 'bout puttin an' end to all this guff when headlights come shinin through the kitchen winduh. Jody May leaps up from her maw's rockin chair an' blows out the light closest to er. I get up an' go 'round to the kitchen to do the same, hopin it wasn't the lights that triggered whoever the fuck's out ere to head this way in the first place, an' just a bad coincidence.

Cain't do much bout the far, but I toss a couple scoops a ash we use for the outdoor shitter awn top, tryna smother it best I can. Just glad it's too dark out fer anyone to see smoke from the chimbley. Small favors an' the like.

I grab the binoculars off the hook near the winduh an' plant em over my nose. Takes a bit to get the focus but when I do I see a car out front of the gate, which is locked. I fixed the fence but it'd be easy nuff for someone who ain't dimwitted like em critters to get over it, just like Tom did that day a couple months back.

Jody May goes, "Who is it?" She's so close er breath tickles the back of my neck.

"Cain't say from here," I tell er. The dumb sonsabitches got the dome light awn in their li'l sedan, an' I see two up front an' maybe one or more smaller ones in the back, but I cain't tell if it's someone we know. "Don't recognize the car, anyways."

That ain't good, of course. Means folks are reachin these parts all the way out from the city. City folk who made it this far without getting they're asses kilt might be smarter'n most, but they still city folk. Me an' Jody May don't got the time to be hodin nobody's hands, an' we ain't 'bout to get ourselves kilt helpin out a stranger.

The driver shuts the door behind hisself an' starts headin for the house. "Shit, he's climbin the fence."

Jody May grabs my shoulder. She's so tense I can feel it in er hand.

I gotta pull the focus to see the guy's face as he gets closer. Skinny guy, dark sweater—hard to tell the color in the moonlight, when ever'thang's a shade of gray—an' a pair of those round John Lennon glasses intellectual types like to wear like it might help em see their own farts wall they sniffin em. He adjusts em awn his nose as he reaches the steps, then starts pattin himself down like he jes walked though a cobweb, but it's prob'ly to make himself more presentable, less like one of em critters.

I set down the binoculars by the sink an' grab the 20-gauge from the broom closet headin fer the door. Rosco's got up from his bed an' sittin by the door, waggin is tail. I gotta push im out the way to open it.

Jody May watches me anxiously.

"Hello?" come a real nervous voice from outside. "I saw your lights. My wife an' I are lookin fer a safe place to spend the night," he goes, only he don't say it like that exactly, he sounds like a college professor, prob'ly from up Stanton way.

"Hello?" he says, loud nuff I hafta worry 'bout him wakin up Mellie in the bedroom, so I open the door, figgerin they ain't no use pretendin we ain't home, like when em Mormons from over'n Wallis County used to come 'round the house, an' Jody May don't wanna offend em by lettin me tell em to go screw. I point the shottie at this fella, an' his hands go shootin up in the air, his eyes just 'bout buggin outta his head.

"I'm not bit, I'm not bit!" he says, real quick, like he musta had practice.

"Be that as it may, ain't no room at the inn," I go. "Plenty of empty houses up the road."

"Please," he says, lowerin his hands a ways. "We're tired, an' low awn gas. We really could just use a place to spend the night an' some gas if you can spare it, then we'll be awn our way."

"They got kids, Bent," Jody May says. She lowers em binoculars an' gives me a look like she used to when she wanted me to take er to the city to watch a movie or get a new dress at the Family Dollar, which wasn't often seein as she's simple folk like me, but nuff that I know the look.

She wants me to let em in.

"Y-yeah," the fella says. "Two boys. Five an' three." He starts lowerin his arms, gettin comfy, so I jab the shottie at im just to remind im whose land he's standin on. His hands shoot right back up to the sky.

"*Bent*," Jody May says, way she does when she don't like me bein stubborn. "They got *kids*," she says again, stressin the word *kids*.

"So do we," I remind er sternly. "An' we cain't protect er with strangers in the house."

"They'll freeze out ere overnight. Just fer tonight, Bent."

The guy nods real eager like he's already got a space awn the floor picked out fer his sleepin bag. He don't know how quick I could put a round of buckshot tween his eyes an' make Jody May's point moot.

But I don't. What I see in er eyes is what I was thankin em couple weeks back. Who gon' share this world with Mellie when me'n er maw meet our Maker? What's the point of all this if we ain't leavin nothin behind for the kids?

I lower the shotgun to my side. "All right," I go. "But just one night then yer own yer way."

"Of course, one night," he goes, then heads back down the porch to get his fambly.

Jody May points with er chin, meanin she wants me to go with im to make sure he gets em all right an' gets back in one piece. I go, of course I go. I'd do just 'bout anythin for Jody May, which has become painfully obvious at the moment.

Puttin our lives at risk for a bunch of city folk. I gotta be outta my damn mind.

I tell Rosco to stay awn the porch an' trudge down the steps after the guy, thankin back to those couple weeks ago when I was thankin 'bout endin it all an' kinda wishin I had. Not really, but I got a bad feelin it'd spare us some heartbreak if I'd done it then an' we went out awn our own terms.

"Name's Thom," the guy says, glancin back at me—or more accurately, at the shotgun—as he drags his feet along awn the dirt road.

"I knew a Tom," I tell im.

"Oh yeah?"

"Yeah. Played ball with im in school. Heckuva guy. He come up awn my property couple months back an' I shot im in the head."

"You..." The guy stumbles an' catches hisself 'fore he can fall. "Had he turned?"

"No sir."

Thom adjusts his glasses. "But he was bit."

"Found that out after."

"So why didn't you just shoot me?"

"'Cause Jody May tode me not to."

Thom eyes me suspiciously as we reach the gate. I use the key awn the lock an' swang it wide so he can pull the car awn through.

"Thank you," he says with a nod.

"Don't thank me, I ain't decided if I'm gon' shoot you or not just yet."

He nods again an' scurries off to the car.

I can see when he climbs in an' the dome light comes on—rookie move not pullin the bulb, but I'll warn im of it when they get to the house—ere's three of em in ere. Wife an' two boys, just like he said. They look scared, an' who can blame em? Even if ere wasn't no critters out ere in the dark, bein from the city they prob'ly still ain't used to seein fellas with guns who ain't army. I doubt they even got one fer emselfs. Prob'ly tell me they was pacifists if I offered one, which I won't.

I follow em up the road to the house. Least he's smart nuff to turn off the runnin lights this time, an' least the car's ode nuff he can. Jody May's got a light flickerin in the house now so it's easier to see where they's headin. Once we get ere'n Thom an' his wife get out, I tell him 'bout the dome light an' he flicks it off quickly.

"Good thankin," he goes.

I nod an' head up to the house wall the two of em gather up the boys. Rosco greets us at the door, sniffin up a storm 'side Jody May. "Wait," I tell em. Rosco sniffs each an' ever one of em—the younger of the two boys shies away from im an' th'other sticks out is han' palm out like yer s'posed to—an' Rosco don't smell nothin so I let em all in, despite my better judgment.

"It's just so nice to see friendly faces," Jody May says.

I'm 'bout to tell er not to get used to it but I check myself an' just head awn over to my chair, wall Jody May ushers em all inside an' they go through all their innerductions like this was some fancy social gatherin 'stead of a bunch of folk hidin away in a farmhouse in a world fulla death.

"So, you've been huntin em?" Jessa, Thom's wife, says to me. "We haven't seen any for five, ten miles, isn't that right, Thom?"

Thom nods. He sips awn the hot cocoa Jody May whipped up for em an' the kids. The boys're asleep awn the floor by the far, where Rosco usually sleeps. Jessa was worried bout lettin em sleep ere but I put up the screen so sparks won't fly at em an' burn em up in their li'l sleepin bags, so she thanked me an' let em. Better'n my idea to get the lot of em spend the night with the pigs in the barn, I s'pose. Rosco's moanin an' pawin away in his sleep 'side my chair, pretty much over my feet.

"Yup," I say.

Jessa looks at me like she's 'spectin me to elaborate. When I don't she turns to er husband.

"You don't find that..." He pauses a sec, like he's deliberatin, or maybe just fer effect. "...troublin?" he says, finally.

"In what way?" I ask.

"They were your friends an' neighbors."

"*Thom...*" his wife says, remindin me of how Jody May said my name when I was contemplatin leavin him out ere awn the porch, an' that reminds me no matter how different we all might be, in some fundamental ways we all the same. Kumbaya an' all that.

"If yer askin was it difficult to kill my friends an' neighbors, th'answer is they was already dead."

"Except Tom," he goes.

I nod. "'Cept Tom. But he was bit, an' his wife an' kids, too. An' I put em outta they misery like I hope someone'd do fer me'n mine, if we got bit. I got a fambly to protect, just like yew folks. I figger ye musta done yer share a thangs yew'da found 'troublin' before."

The two of em share a look that tells me they did, but I don't need the look or a reply to know they had. Wouldn'ta made it this far if they hadn't.

"Was this a workin farm?" Thom asks, eager to change the subject. "Before," he adds, as if it ain't implied.

"We grow burley tobacco," Jody May says proudly, lookin at me with a soft smile. "Most farms 'round here stopped growin it durin the decline but Bentley an' me—" She only ever uses my full name when we got comp'ny. "—we still get by."

"Somebody gotta grow it," I says.

I see Thom rise a bit in his chair, an' his wife reacts by squeezin his knee like she knows he's bout to get hisself into a scuffle an' she don't want no part of it.

"Thank ye again so much for lettin' us in," she goes, an' Thom relaxes into Mawmaw Mellie's ode rocker. "An' for the meal."

"Always happy to have comp'ny," Jody May goes.

"Welp, I'm gon' catch some shut eye," I says, gettin up. Rosco jumps up soon as I move an' shakes his head, makin his collar jingle an' wakin up the smallest boy. Th'oder one's fast asleep with his thumb stuck in his mouth. Shoulda been trained outta that by now I figger, but I ain't gon' tell em how to raise their boy. If they want him to grow up a sissy, that's their business.

Jody May gets up from the sofa 'side Jessa. It's a pullout, an' Jessa an' er husband'll be fine out here. Jody May reminds em 'bout the linens an' a heavy blanket she's set out awn the table for em, an' tells em if they have any problems in the night that we're "right ere in the next room," which is funny 'cause ere's only two rooms an' the septic shitter, so where else we gon' be?

"Go ahead an' put another log awn the far if ye get too code," I tell em, tryna be a li'l bit hospitable. For city folk they seem to mostly got their heads awn straight, even though it's pretty clear Thom an' me got a few disagreements 'bout the way things are or ought to be.

"Thank ye Bent," Thom says. "We really appreciate yuns lettin us stay."

I nod. "Welp, just don't make me regret it."

"We won't," says Jessa.

Rosco's sittin by the boys, waggin his tail. I gotta slap my leg to get him off his keister. "C'mon, boy."

"He likes em," Jessa goes.

An' it's true. Rosco always had a fondness fer children, boys 'specially. Figger I'll let em thow the ball 'round for him a bit in the mornin 'fore we send em packin.

"G'night," Jody May says.

"Goodnight," Thom an' Jessa say back.

NEXT MORNIN, Rosco goes shootin down the road, followin the ol' rubber ball as it bounces, paws kickin up dust.

It's eight A.M. an' we've all had a good breakfast of bacon an' eggs, no toast though 'cause that's one of the first things to go bad. Em boys got an appetite, which is good to see, an' even better knowin they ain't vegan or allergic to gluten or some other New Age shit. They just reg'lar kids tryna cope with the shit han' they got dealt, an' it's good to see em laughin an' horsin around even though I'd rather put em to work gatherin eggs or feedin the sows whose sister they ate fer breakfast. Figger kids should know where their food comes from, an' that's somethin Mellie's gon' learn early. Thom made a wisecrack about farm-to-table wall Jody May was servin us up, an' I made a point of tellin him it's the folks who know how to farm an' hunt gon' inherit the Earth, if they last that long, 'cause canned food an' Twinkies ain't gon' keep ferever. Gotta start thankin long-term, 'specially with kids to worry 'bout.

"I heard ere's people workin awn a cure," Jessa said to that.

Jody May looks to me when she did, 'cause we had this discussion a hundred times if we had it once.

"Whether they is or whether they ain't don't make a lick of difference to the here an' now, does it?" I went. "They could make a cure tomorrow an' we still gon' need fresh food today. Not like Oscar Meyer's gon' be puttin hot dogs an' code cuts awn yer table fer a wall, if ever. Nope, it's back to the days of huntin' an' gath-erin' fer some time yet, I figger. An' the quicker ye get used to it, the better off yew an' yer kids'll be."

Jessa made to argue, but this time Thom put a han' awn er knee under the table.

"Yer right," he said. "Do ye, um, know somewhere we could get—"

"*Thom*," the wife scoded.

"What? Bent's right, we need to start thankin long term. Squash rackets'n fryin pans'll only hode em off so long."

"We've done well so far."

"We've been *lucky*," Thom said. "We cain't keep 'pendin awn the kindness of strangers forever, Jess."

Well, Jody May got up an' started cleanin up plates off the table then, an' the discussion petered off. Wall the women washed the dishes, me an' Thom an' the boys went out front to chuck the ball for Rosco.

"I need a gun," Thom goes after a wall of just standin 'round in silence, watchin the boys play.

"Yup," I say.

"Is that somethin... I mean could I maybe borrow...?"

"Tell ye what," I go. "I gotta head into town awn a erran' anyways, I could pick ye up somethin if ye want."

"I could come with ye."

"Nope," I says. "Ye'd just slow me down."

I see that took the wind outta his sails, but he don't argue. "That's fair."

"Army gathered up all the guns'n ammo from the hardware store, but I happen to know where the cache is."

"They'll just let y in?"

"Don't got much choice in the matter considerin all em sonsabitches're deader'n Judas Iscariot."

Thom raises an eyebrow at me. His youngest boy, Peter, chucks the ball far as he can an' Rosco goes boltin down the road, chasin after it. "Ye know that fer sure?" Thom goes.

"Kilt the last one of em maybe three four weeks ago an' I ain't seen nor heard nothin from that base since. Maybe the rest went underground. I figger that's where our shitheel president is, 'long with the rest of his fat cat cronies. Deep under some mountain somewheres, waitin this whole thing out. If we're lucky they all died with the rest of em, flushed down the Great Cosmic Crapper like the turds they are. Or *was*. But we ain't been lucky yet."

"I like that," Thom goes. "The Great Cosmic Crapper."

"Well, ye can use it if ye like."

Rosco rolls over awn his back for Peter. The boy rubs Rosco's belly, an' Rosco's back leg starts kickin. Boy musta hit his sweet spot. "Daddy," the oder boy goes, comin back to us with the slobbery ball in his hand. "Can we get a dog?"

"I'll thank awn it," Thom goes, then he gives me a look that says he's seen some of the shit I have. That Rosco's prob'ly the only good dog still out ere an' the rest are bit or worse.

"I truly appreciate ye helpin us out, Bent."

"Don't thank nothin of it," I go.

GETTIN A GUN FER THOM AN' his fambly ain't no big ordeal like I made it out to be, I just prefer to be alone with Rosco an' my thoughts sometimes. Big thoughts this mornin, 'bout the nature of this fuckin virus an' what the hell it's fittin to do once we all either got bit or we're gone. It's a virus's purpose to be fruitful an' multiply, like the Bible says 'bout those of us God created in His own image. But when it's multiplied to the point it cain't multiply no further, what then? What good's a planet fulla corpses to a virus? It's already spread to the dogs an' cats an' rodents an' whatnot. What's next? Take the deer an' the pigs? The birds outta the damn trees? Can the world even go awn livin with all the animals gone, just the bugs an' the trees to keep it comp'ny?

I like to thank ere's nuff survivors out ere to keep the world turnin. Thom an' Jessa say they heard ere's a quarantine zone down in Atlanta still up an' runnin but I doubt it, an' I made my doubts clear. Don't want Jody May gettin any thoughts 'bout riskin what we got—which both Thom an' Jessa agree is a lot, compared to folks they seen awn the road—to try an' find some supposed virus-free paradise that prob'ly don't exist outside of rumor, an' if it does exist it's likely no better'n the conditions folks faced inside the Superdome durin Katrina, or when the army ran Praytor. Halfta be a damn fool to give up the farm an' all the free pickins we can ask for in town for a pipe dream. Though I suppose after a time even what we got in Praytor'll be gone, used up an' tossed in a heap out behind the barn where we buried Jody May's maw once the army wasn't 'round no more to prevent it.

Ere's plenty of guns to choose from at the army cache. They went 'round door-to-door collectin handguns an' ammo an' only left us with a single rifle or a shotgun to protect the house. Figger they didn't want us comin after em if things slipped outta their control, which they did just 'bout lickety-split.

I grab a Glock-17 for Thom—figger it's a good pistol for someone who's prob'ly never shot so much as a squirrel in his life—an' a couple boxes of 9mm hollow point rounds. Figger if he manages to hit a critter, a hollow point'll stop the sumbitch in its tracks long nuff for em to make a break for it if he cain't get it in the head. We'll pop off a few rounds out in the back nine when I get back, show him how to handle the thing so he don't fuck up an' blow his own head off or shoot on of them boys.

I grab a camo Desert Eagle I'm pretty sure b'longed to Jerry Ester who used to run the army surplus store—army fellas musta pried it from his code dead hands—an' pop a couple boxes of .50 AE rounds into the duffel with it. Never had much use for a pistol 'fore, but after that close call in close quarters at the hardware store I been thankin 'bout pickin one up, an' I figger, when in Rome, do as the Romans did. Be nice to have somethin small that'll put up a stink if one of em gets that close again.

Rosco takes a piss awn the army barricade awn our way back to the truck like he always does, markin his territory, like he ain't the only domesticated dog fer a meeyun miles. It's a nice day fer late fall. Chill in the air but the sun warm awn the skin, with only a few of em big puffy dark clouds way off in the distance. Gotta take life's li'l pleasures wall you can, considerin how few it offers these days.

I drive back to the farm in a weird kinda bliss. Watchin em boys playin ball an' tusslin with Rosco reminded me of the good times I had with Curtis when I was their age. Good to see life back awn the farm, even if it is only for a short spell. I got a CCR tape playin with an arm stuck out the winduh, an' Rosco's hangin his head out awn his side, big ol' tongue hangin out, baskin in that mornin sunshine. Cain't help but let a big goofy grin spread 'cross my face.

Tape ain't playin loud but it's nuff I don't hear the car horn up ahead til we whip 'round the corner, then I turn down the player an' it's loud as a siren, one long bleat pealin out across Hell's half acre, nuff to wake the dead, as maw used to say.

Thom's sedan's in the road up ahead, half in the ditch. Gate's swung wide.

"Jesus jumped-up fuckin Christ," I mutter, an' Rosco starts bayin out the winduh, way he does when he catches scent of one of em critters. All the bliss I had comin back here's gone now, took over by pure unfiltered dread. Somethin fuckin bad's happened here, an' Thom's car in the road is just the tip of the iceberg.

I step awn the brakes, kickin up dust behind Thom's sedan. Get my rifle at the ready an' leap out the door. Rosco tries to get out my side but I tell him to stay an' close the door behind me to make sure he does as he's tode.

Thom's face first awn the horn, that's how come it's blarin. I train the gun awn him as I step around to his winduh, which is smashed in. The li'lun, Peter, lies curled up in the front passenger seat. Both of em is covered in blood. I move in quick an' grab Thom by the shoulder an' yank him back. The silence closes in. Thom's neck is torn open an' he gurgles blood. He's openin an' closin his mouth like a fish outta water, like he wants to talk but he cain't. Then he goes, "Peter... it bit Peter... down at the creek."

I can tell that just by lookin at em. Bit em both, by the look, but I don't got time to ask how, or just what in the blue fuck they was doin down at the creek when I tode em 'spressly to stay at the got damn house.

"Where's Jody May?"

"The house..." he goes, then slumps to his side, fallin over his boy.

"Goddammit," I go. I consider puttin a bullet in the two of em so I don't hafta deal with em later, but instead I hurry back to the truck. Rosco jumps out the second I get the door open, an' he goes tearin up the road like when he was chasin that ball of his little over'n hour ago. Jesus Christ, how could this happen? What the fuck was they doin at the creek? Looks like Thom drove off with his kid an' smashed through the gate from the skid marks in the dirt. Maybe they was headin fer town, lookin fer me in a hurry. Which means ere's prob'ly a worse situation waitin fer me at the house.

I tode er. I tode Jody May we cain't go helpin ever'one who comes 'round no more. *This is what happens.* Ere's a special corner in Hell reserved fer Good Samaritans these days. I just hope to Christ she had the wherewithal to lock erself an'

Mellie in the bedroom or the shitter, an' all that happened is what I just seen. That the rest of em is safe in the house, or at least my girls are. Please, let what's back ere in the road be the end of it.

I know it ain't true soon's I get close nuff to the house to see the front door left wide open. Ain't no way Jody May'd leave it like that if she weren't in deep shit or worse. An' ain't a sound comin from inside, which could be good or bad. Rosco's growlin awn the porch, standin by the door waitin fer me.

I head awn up the stairs an' the first sight that greets me is a relief. Ere's a man awn the floor, wearin one of em orange huntin vests an' camo. The big fry pan's lyin aside im in a big ol' pool of blood, an' he ain't got a head. Whoever did im in, an' I'm guessin it was one of the mothers, considerin the violence they done to him, maybe Jessa for him takin er boy from er, smashed his head to a pulp awn the floor.

"Jody May?" I call out.

"In here," she goes, real quiet from behind the bedroom door. Sounds like she's cryin. I just 'bout feel like cryin myself, an' I ain't cried since we put Curtis down when I was ten.

Rosco's standin at my side, his hackles up.

One of em's bit in ere.

"Jessa an' the boy in ere with ye?"

"They're dead, Bent," she goes, weepin between er words. "They're all dead."

I bite back my anger an' reach for the door. It's locked.

Rosco growls.

"Ye gotta let me in, Jody May."

Her sobbin gets louder. Don't sound like she's makin er way to the door.

"Peter ran down to the creek," she goes. "Jessa went after him a-an' Thom, an' it followed em back. *It followed em back*, Bent!"

"*Jody May*," I says again. "Ye gotta let me in or I cain't do nothin for ye."

She's sobbin an' shiverin in ere, an' the sobs an' shivers get closer to the door. I hear the lock turn an' I open the door.

My heart just 'bout burst when I see she's covered in blood. Jody May's th'only gal I ever loved. Took er to prom an' married er soon's er maw gave us er blessin. Tried for eight years to have a baby, Jody May prayin just 'bout ever night for God to bless us with a child of our own.

"Are ye bit?"

"I ain't bit, Bent. I swear to God, I ain't bit."

An' even though Jody May don't swear to God if she don't mean it, Rosco's growls sing a different tune.

"Are ye *bit*, goddammit?"

She shakes er head, big tears spillin down er cheeks. Then she looks at the crib.

Mellie's been silent all this time. She don't cry much at all, 'cept when she's done a mess in er diaper, or when er maw'n me raise our voices. But she ain't cryin now, an' our voices are raised just 'bout as high as they ever been.

I step over to the crib an' the sight tears my heart out.

Li'l baby Mellie, lyin in a pool of blood. She's breathin, but er pudgy li'l cheek's been bit right off. Fucker musta bit er in Jody May's arms wall she was fightin'm off, that's how come he ain't got a head no more. Jody May done pulverized it.

I'm cryin my own self. 'Cause they ain't nothin we can do for Mellie, not now. Thom thought he could save Peter, I figger, an' the boy tore his throat out wall they was drivin to town to find me. Jessa an' th'other boy musta got bit somewhere 'tween the creek an' the house, an' we cain't help em neither. Ain't no vaccine, ain't no amputation gon' put a stop to it. Only way to help em now is with a bullet.

"W-we have to," Jody May says, lookin down at our girl.

I nod. Much as I don't wanna b'lieve it, we gotta do what's right, an' what's right is to send li'l Mellie back to Jesus.

Jody May picks up one of the pillows from the crib, the one with the ladybirds awn it, an' she raises it over our angel's precious li'l head.

Ain't nothin we can do now but pray it's over quick.

"I can do it if ye cain't," I tell er.

"No," Jody May goes. "It should be me." She cain't even look when she pushes the ladybird pillow down over Mellie's face, smotherin the life out of er. The life she gave er. Takin it away like I shoulda done em weeks back when I thought of it, spare us all a world of hurt. Maybe even Thom an' Jessa an' the boys'd still be alive. Woulda drove right past the farmhouse, maybe found some gas at one of the places down the road an' holed up fer the night an' moved awn in the mornin, makin their way down to their fictional paradise in Atlanta.

Jody May pushes down, an' li'l Mellie start cryin, soft an' muffled by the ladybirds. The three of us bawlin our eyes out, shuttin the winduh the Lord opened when he closed the door.

That's when Rosco lunges.

I shoulda seen it comin. Rosco loves that girl, even more'n me'n er maw. He'd do anythin to protect er, even if she was bit. An' he done proved it now, chompin down awn Jody May's calf. She wails an' drops the pillow, an' Rosco hunkers down awn the floor with a hound dog look, knowin he done wrong.

Jody May flops down awn the bed where she kneels to pray. She strips a pillowcase off an' presses it to the wound awn er leg. Blood soaks through the white cotton fast, an' Rosco's got blood drippin from his mouth wall he pants, waitin to take his lickin.

Then I see it. I musta been so outta my mind with horror it didn't even register when I come in the room.

"Jody May, your arm," I go.

She looks down at it, an' er eyes go wide like she didn't even notice she was bit from all the commotion, with all the blood coverin er from bashin in that critter's head out'n the kitchen.

She's bit. Our li'l angel's bit, too. An' Rosco, the dumb sumbitch, he done bit Jody May.

I hate to say it, but looks like our luck finally done run out. God decided to call in all His debts, an' this time, He ain't gon' take nothin awn credit.

I cock my rifle an' grit my teeth, decidin awn which one of em's gon' get the first bullet.

Duncan Ralston is the author of the cult smash-hit Woom and Ghostland and more than 15 other books that aren't the cult smash-hit Woom or Ghostland. His debut collection was blurbed positively by the legendary Jack Ketchum. His latest, Pedo Island Bloodbath, has been nominated for a 2024 Splatterpunk Award for Best Novel.

AFTERWORD
FROM THE DESK OF DUNCAN RALSTON

The editor would like to thank all of the good dogs out there for making our lives richer, for helping us get around, for comforting us, for helping us work, for teaching us empathy, for protecting us when we're in danger.

I'd also like to thank each and every one of these amazing authors for trusting me with your work. It's been a long while since I've published an anthology, and I hope I did your stories justice.

And of course, thanks to the readers, without whom efforts like this would not be needed. You keep us writing. We'd probably do it without you, but it'd be a lot less rewarding.

And a special thank you to Silvio, the grumpy li'l miniature Schnauzer who was with me for eleven years and got me through some of the toughest times of my life. Miss you, buddy.

D.R.
November, 2024

MORE FROM SWP

For more delicious dark fiction, please visit
www.duncanralston.com and
www.shadowworkpublishing.com.

9 781988 819488